Veleno

Michelle Novak

ISBN-13: 978-1523961948

ISBN-10: 1523961945

Printed by CreateSpace, An Amazon.com Company

Cover Design: SelfPubBookCovers.com/houchi

Author's Website:
inspiredbyvenice.org

For
Jessica,
Heather,
Elizabeth
and
Kelly.

My
strong,
beautiful,
intelligent
sisters.

The Garden

Mafalda was with her sisters on the terrace roof garden. She had a nagging feeling that this wasn't quite right, but the unbidden laughter coming from Fina, Noemi and Paola played so beautifully in her ears that any uneasy thoughts kept flitting away. All four of the ladies wore long golden dresses, different in each their own way, which caressed their slipper-covered toes at the hems. Fina, the oldest at 20, reclined on a wooden chair at the edge of their private Eden between two potted citrus trees. Her naturally brown hair dyed blond, hung over the marble enclosure behind the head of her seat, cascading for all the passersby in their gondolas on the canal below to admire. It was lately her habit to drench her tresses in any number of concoctions and then expose her head to the sun on fine days.

The third born at 17, Noemi, stood elegantly tall while blowing bubbles out of a copper hoop attached to the end of a slim rod. Her auburn hair was only half-captured in a golden threaded net; errant curls stirred freely over her shoulders. After each dip of the small circlet into a pewter bowl filled with foamy water, she would make explosively surprised or perplexed looks

1

at the passing orbs carried off in the wind.

Paola was delighted with Noemi's acting and giggled more effervescently than the delicate bubbles. The youngest had always been slight. She sat meekly; orange blossom weaved in a crown upon her head and a silver plate on her lap. The scent of the freshly sliced green apples resting there was so telling of her elfin presence; the black-haired, dark-eyed, forest-looking creature that she was, loved tart green apples. The others found them too sour.

Mafalda buoyantly stood from her own chair in order to seek out, pop and react to spoiled bubbles so as to delight their little sister further. Instantly however, she felt stuck in place where she stood, her body incomprehensibly heavy when it was before so light. The warm breeze seemed too, to lose its soothing qualities in an instant, the sting of ice carried in its touch. The skies were darker then, in too quick a time. As she looked to Fina, it was clear that her sister had recognized the change along with her. The eldest stood instantly, letting her long damp hair fall to her back as she gazed out past the happy garden and scanned the city of Venice below. When she turned back, there was a sincere fear in her eyes, one she'd normally have kept from the younger girls.

Veleno

The cold was now almost too much to bear, creeping toward the bones. Mafalda felt ill as she watched Fina fix her stare directly in her direction. And though she did not see or hear her say the words, she distinctly felt her say, "Open your eyes Mafalda. Open them *now*!"

Mafalda

Pain. That was all that echoed in the dark places of her mind as her lids slowly fluttered open, her eyeballs feeling like frozen grapes stinging in their sockets. When fully opened, she observed one lone white cloud float slowly through a blue sky. It was only when it was out of view that the smell slipped up over her like a violent restraint, making her gag and sit up.

Unable to comprehend where she sat, she spent a moment dazed and looking at her legs, which were covered only with a thin white shift and stretching out before her. The material seemed immobile, frozen in place to every change in her form; she could see pearly skin below the linen, much too pale.

Looking to her feet, she found them bare and deathly white; her usually well-kept toenails were blue, her toes unmoving. Just beyond, the frozen face of a female with eyes wide open in a dead stare rested unmoving, appearing in just the right position to bite her exposed feet. The stone face looked to have a black eye. Sucking in what air she could, readying a scream, the excruciating expansion of icy ribs pushed a choke and several coughs out instead, causing her to lean forward forcefully. Mafalda was in more agony than

4

she had ever considered possible.

Sitting right again, she tried to steady her breathing as she looked around her with eyes wide and lips trembling. Fear instantly made her number than her frosty bearings; dead bodies posed frozen about her, a thin layer of snow covering them all as though sugar had been sifted from above. For a moment, she was confused with how the snow did not lay the same upon her own stuck profile as it did on the others, but soon realized that it was from life. She was alive, warmer than the rest, if only but by a degree. The light snow that had fallen over her had melted.

Blinking, she peered at her hands. Where richly gemmed bands of gold once encircled her delicate tanned fingers, only ghastly pale skin shown. Not a single adornment where was always a trinket, even whilst she bathed or slept. Her usually long and manicured fingernails were broken and dirty. As her eyes moved up to one of her piteously thin wrists, just along the fine lace that cuffed the sleeve of her shift, she cringed at a black-and-blue bruise peeking out. Moving to lift the sleeve, she found what was a raised round the size of a large coin. It was a lanced and deflating sore, sliced down the middle. The remains of black blood crusted along the line of the cut, and the wound was yet red in places amidst the bruising.

Letting the sleeve fall, she assessed her pains while observing her surroundings. Her lower half felt numb in places and stung severely in others while her torso ached as though it had met with a severe clubbing. Breathing was heavy and laborious. Though she couldn't much feel her face, her ears burned. Mafalda reached up to touch her long dark-blond hair and found it tied up, but with strands loose and dampened from the snow. There was grit in the feel, sand or dirt. Moving her fingers just under her ear upon her neck, she found yet another bump that made her grimace by the slightest touch. Softly pushing on it, a warm liquid met her fingertips and ran down into the cavern of her palm. Inspecting her hand, she nearly fainted to find green-yellow pus and fresh blood; a bubo that had just burst or had previously been lanced and was draining.

Making to wipe her hand in the snow aside her, she uncovered a man's large paw frozen solid. The fingertips were completely black. Mafalda shuddered in horror while scanning what she now understood to be a pit, not too deep or large, but big enough that she could not see out over the edge of it while in her seated place. She was thankful for the thin layer of snow;

should she have met the full scene without it, she would have succumbed to shock. The unnatural lumps from unmoving arms and legs and partially exposed faces were everywhere; she thought an appendage moved ever so slightly in places, but only for a second. It was completely silent. Again the hideously repugnant stink overcame her, which she now recognized as coming from what slumbered below, a smell which had the day been warmer, would have been incomprehensible.

In all, it was only a few minutes from waking that her scrambled thoughts started to become a vague recollection for just how she must have come to be in this hellish situation. She wanted to yell out for help, but immediately thought better of it. She'd heard about the *pizzicamorti*, collectors of the dead and the *beccamorti*, the gravediggers who buried them. She knew that when the plague came to Venice, those chosen for such grim work were an especially ruthless lot. It wasn't a good idea to meet with one if she could help it.

Suddenly she recalled sitting on the rooftop of her family's *palazzo*, prestigiously situated so close to the *Canal Grando*. There was warmth and laughter, and her sisters were all there. Mafalda knew that this was no memory however. Though they had indeed spent many days lounging in that lofty garden, the one place out-of-doors where respectable noble-born ladies could relax away from the public eye, summer had passed months ago. It had only been a dream, a sweet delusion to soothe her as she laid freezing.

Just then she recalled the moment of Fina's plea for her to wake, while at the same time reaching one cold hand along the back of her neck where something felt snagged in a tangled strand of hair. She immediately forgot the thought of her sister as she discovered that there was one remaining adornment, a gold necklace strung around her frail neck. It smarted as she tugged at it, freeing it from the hair where it was caught and then pulling the front of the chain from out of her shift. The gold string sparkled in the sunlight, and at its end still remained the beautiful white pearl, an object of great importance to her. About to tuck it back into place and begin forming thoughts for how she might pull herself to the edge of the mass grave, she heard a noise and looked up to see that she was not the only one to have taken inventory of the pearl.

Orso

The name Orso meant 'bear', which was exactly how his daughters thought of him. To say nothing that he was an immense man, he was also very powerful. All of the city's nobles esteemed him and avoided becoming out of favor with him. It was his usual custom to be irritable and loud; the force of his voice echoed through the great marble halls of his palace and the servants clambered out of the way. Though he was regularly away to keep a close watch on his landward estate and trading monopolies, which yielded regular and sometimes enormous profits, when home he was the hibernating sort of creature who the girls rarely saw. When they did, it was usually during one of the great occasions thrown in the *palazzo*, when once every so many months, Venice's elite were invited to partake in Orso's notorious hospitality. Though all great families did as much, the House of Orso had a reputation for opulent hosting.

He had a beautiful wife, Mirella, a name with the meaning 'to admire'. On such occasions that the bear opened his doors, he would drink copious amounts of rare wine, eat the most delectable seafood that the Adriatic offered and would laugh loudly enough to rattle the windows. And though it was some 30 years since the death of the English King, Henry VIII, there was occasionally a noble of Queen Elizabeth's court who passing through Venice and visiting his house, likened Orso to that full and extravagant person. His wife was indeed a comely woman and he liked nothing better than to watch her dance before a blaze, hearthside in their dining hall, as she honored their various male guests as partner. From there, he could favorably view her body silhouetted by the fire and grew lustier with each courtly dance. He made no excuses when catching his wife in his grip, would squeeze her rump over her exquisite gowns and with impassioned kisses, would leave her blushing before their guests and servants. However, no one ever found his hot behavior lewd. He was considered a fair businessman, a benevolent citizen, and generous to all; one could easily overlook his bouts of salaciousness, ill temper or the smashing of the occasional glass goblet.

And despite his hardly participating in the upbringing of his four daughters, he seemed to love them well enough and provided them with an affluent, comfortable living. Furthermore, he had never been known to speak of any disappointment in never having gotten a son, something other noblemen demanded of their wives. Orso seemed satisfied with his brood of girls and no one was ever brave enough to question whether he didn't desire a male heir. He was also suspected to be very much in love with his wife. It was even rumored that he had never taken a courtesan or wench, though many a soft set of thighs in the city would have lined up for just a few of his gold coins.

During one Carnival, the *palazzo* hosted an enormous feast and masquerade. After all of the guests were gone and floating home through the snaking canals in their gondolas, and the servants had been dismissed to their rest, Mafalda spied her parents yet sitting at table before the fire. They were cooing like doves and laughing pleasantly. That was what she wanted for herself, a marriage struck from love. It was just a few quick years after Mafalda made that wish, that far stranger fates were cast for each of Orso's daughters.

Fina

Fina knew that something was astir. Though she could never have called her mother unkind, it was a fact that Mirella had never been particularly tender towards any of the girls. It was only at certain times that there seemed to be *some* affection, but it was obvious to her when her mother was making a show of it to visitors and neighbors. Then, it felt like just an act to make herself look doting and proud of such fine daughters. No, it was only at very *rare* times when Mirella was alone with the girls that she might begin to laugh with them, sharing some story from before she was married, or joining in for a few moments of leaping with the girls as they practiced with their dance master, that she seemed sincere. There might even be a kiss on the forehead, a squeeze to the hand, or the sweeping away of a wisp of hair from a daughter's face. But it never lasted long enough, leaving the girls ever hungry for Mirella's deeper attention.

Now, things seemed even colder. Their father had been away and for much longer than was usual. Fina noticed that their mother was acting strangely. There was that quibbling with a tradesman who had come to call for his pay. It was odd, for Mirella was usually indifferent to even large expenses. Then there was a demand for one of her lady's maids to take down an elaborate hairstyle that the poor servant had spent an hour working; she'd screeched for her to start again. Their mother was always beautiful; Fina couldn't understand what the provocation had been.

One evening very late, she'd spied her mother masked and under cloak, exiting the *palazzo* and entering a gondola. The boat carried a *felze*, a cabin that sheltered her in the belly of the vessel. Fina had no way of knowing if anyone else was inside or where she might be going. The next day as she sat stitching with her mother and 19-year-old Mafalda, she inquired but was met with a fierce look, which quickly melted into a tender laugh. Mirella claimed that it was only a friend who had come for a short visit; it was *her* seen leaving at that hour. Of course, this was possible and frequent enough, their home was grand and visitors came and went without notice when it didn't concern Fina. She had only happened to open the shutters from within her chamber to let in some cool air. But she still believed it had been her mother.

Then there was the matter of Noemi, always considered the handsomest. Mirella had been curiously sweet to Noemi of late. Noting how often

Rodolfo (rarely admitted into their home) was being invited to festivities, Fina thought she knew why. The name Rodolfo stood for 'famous wolf'. He embraced the label well, for he was a cringingly direct and cutting young man. Being the son of a very rich merchant, he felt at liberty to be as deliberately condescending as he liked. His father happened also to be Orso's fierce business rival, thus he was not frequently on the guest list unless their father was feeling particularly good willed. Though stealthily, Mirella seemed to be encouraging Noemi to be kind to Rodolfo, directing her to fill his wine goblet, to dance with him or engage him in small conversations, all in the name of being polite to *all* their guests.

Noemi had become flushed when she was found reading a missive. Was there some poison dart amongst her usual letters? They usually only ever contained kind words from her friends or their far-flung Aunt Gostanza. She'd seemed distracted, her green eyes reflecting deep thoughts. She had refolded the paper and claiming that she was tired, had left the room with red curls aswirl. If there *were* letters from Rodolfo entering the house, Fina was certain their father wouldn't approve and that Noemi should tell their mother. It was Mirella's duty to tactfully put a stop to the correspondence, as Orso would want her to do. That was unless their mother was quietly encouraging a union. Fina didn't press Noemi about the agitating letter, fearing their mother was at the heart of it. She cared for her sisters and as the eldest, would intervene for any of them if they were desperate. But crossing one of their marble-hard parents wasn't something she wanted to entertain.

There was also Mirella's refusal to allow Fina to visit her friend, Aurelia. Both highborn daughters, living in *palazzi* separated merely by a few narrow canals, they had been close since they were children. With only a modest and often floundering production in the mining of sea salt, Aurelia's father was not nearly as successful as Orso in keeping his wealth, let alone accumulating more. But though he failed to meet the opulent standards for noble Venetians, he had always done well enough by his family, able to keep them living in their tired, crumbling *palazzo* with fish and wine on the table. Sorrowfully, Aurelia's parents had both died of a fever that washed in like a flash flood under their door. It took her only sibling as well, a smart and gentle younger brother. Though usually to a son or other male relative, with none living, Aurelia now owned her father's property. She felt fortunate that her father hadn't passed down any debts, and she never complained about what little assets had been left to live on. She was proud, but she'd also loved her parents.

Initially Aurelia had welcomed marriage, but soon realized that she'd never be selected to match with another noble family, as she did not have a bulging dowry. Alternatively, the thought of coupling with a man below her noble birth couldn't tempt her, especially as she would have to sell her family's home; no shopkeeper or fisherman would have been able to provide the income to sustain it.

More than once had Fina heard Aurelia scoff at the idea of marrying a tradesman; to toil and birth a poor man's offspring with no certain comforts choked her to consider, she'd said. In spite of her father not having secured great wealth, he *had* been cultivated. Further, he'd allowed Aurelia to be schooled alongside her brother, pleased to see them both learning with a tutor. And as was an esteemed lady's right, she'd also taken the required dance, music and singing lessons, and had excelled. Fortuitously, she was also pleasing to the eye. And so, rising above the wretchedness she'd felt from losing her family, and any endlessly bleak prospects of a future, she became a courtesan. She sold the salt operation and with the income, made many necessary repairs while simultaneously refreshing her accommodations. She cleverly negotiated prices and staged the old dwelling and its small walled garden attractively. Hiring a merry brood of seamstresses, she had her and her mother's old gowns torn apart and reworked to create newer, more captivating fashions. She dyed her hair blond with rather toxic smelling tinctures from the apothecary, and revealed it to the bleaching powers of the sun, as courtesans did.

Mirella had never spoken meanly of Aurelia, either before or after she'd chosen this profession. She herself entertained illustrious and learned courtesans in her home. Of late however, Mirella seemed to come up with irritating wants that kept Fina from her intended plans to see her friend. Only unusual at first, her visits were soon halted altogether when her mother told her outright that she would no longer be permitted the gondola for excursions to that house, and also that Aurelia would not be among their future guests. The very moment she was told, Fina would have rebuked her mother's decision with a fierce argument, but a scream from the heart of the *palazzo* had cut her rebuttal short.

Paola

For a few days, Paola hadn't been feeling well. She'd had headaches, stomachaches and intense pains that would strike her and run down her neck. For several of those nights, she'd had horrible nightmares, finding herself toeing down a cold stone corridor, barefoot, shaking from the chill in only a shift, her black hair damp and clinging to her skin. In one dream, she was carrying a single lit taper without a chamberstick and the hot dripping wax burned her as it met her delicate hand. But in all, she was searching for a way out. There were occasional shrieks or moans, but the sounds came to her muffled after moving through the dense rock walls. She was unable to see whom, or even what creature, was troubled. But she knew, something terrible surrounded her. She'd needed to find her way out, to see resplendent light and smell the sea. Even the quiet flow of a canal would have sounded like an angel's song. She whispered frantic prayers of deliverance in the dreams, words that faltered as she came to a halt before the figure of something large and teetering ahead of her in the darkness. Was it an immense person? A bear?

Paola had once seen a moon bear from Russia

during *Carnevale* being paraded around Piazza San Marco by five chains around its neck and limbs, being guided by dirty, jeering handlers. The beast roared as loudly as the clanging from the Campanile while standing on two feet, and she had been terrified. Nevertheless, squatting down behind the crowd, she'd rolled an apple between the onlookers' feet. It stopped before the animal. Eyeing the object, it went down to all fours and sniffed the fruit. She'd hoped he'd take the gift and be at peace, if only for a moment, but his captors wrestled him onward, the apple's green skin and pulp mashed underfoot of the festival seekers. Days later, she'd learned that the bear had been slain for show by 'valiant' swordsmen, a fate many exotic beasts met for a crowd's pleasure. Alone in her chamber, she'd wept.

Paola would wake from her haunted dreams each time she tried to make out the *thing* that stood just out of view in the darkness. She'd find herself in a cold sweat in her bed, tempted to whine and call out for any of her sisters' smiling faces. But at 15, she knew that she was too old for it. She couldn't explain her symptoms, or the nightmares that overcame her in her sleep; that was unsettling enough. But worse, she'd been experiencing constant uneasiness. It was as though

19

Veleno

something awful was coming, with nothing to stand in its way.

Mirella

All fine wines became acrid in time, sometimes bittering before they could be enjoyed, let alone savored. When a vinegary sip from a rancid bottle recently made its way into her goblet, Mirella quipped under her breath that it tasted like her life.

Almost 25 years had passed since she'd been a maiden abiding within her father's countryside villa in Padua. Fragrant purple Wisteria clung to buildings and the fields were full of hearty vines. The son of the man who oversaw her father's yield had taught her to taste the soil to see if it held the properties to sustain the growth of grapes; she became a girl who knew where to look for survival.

Now, she'd sometimes regard her own girls and a smile would flash upon her lips as she remembered that same ebullient laughter, that innocence and energy, that playfulness that she'd shared with her own sister who'd been just two years older than herself. With loose hair, in light raiment and barefoot, they'd scamper through the vineyard, hiding from one another amongst the fruit. Lying lazily in the sun, they'd smash grapes between their toes.

But her smile would quickly fade to revisit what

had taken place. Destinies were revealed too soon, severing their bond, changing their lives forever. Sadly, it would be just the same for this new generation of daughters, for noble girls were never free. Back in that year of 1551, things were not so very changed from how they were now in 1575. For every nobleman with a great heritage, there were decisions to be made about the future of his family's wealth. These arrangements were never made when a nobleman grew old, but were quickly decided with the birth of each of his children.

The planning for a child's future was rarely emotional, especially not for Severiano, meaning 'stern'. His eldest was a boy, Liborio. Next came a daughter, Lagia. Then there was Mirella. The mother of them all, Paula, had died in childbirth with her fourth child. It had been a male who squalled for just an hour before growing quiet and leaving the world with his mother. He'd never even been given a name. Mirella had baptized her own fourth daughter Paola, after seeing her dark head of hair for the first time. She had been so tiny too, so much like Mirella's mother with her slight frame and raven hair. The names Paula and Paola were but a letter apart.

It had been decided at his birth that should Liborio survive his father, he would inherit all. Any of

Severiano's future sons would be assigned a lifelong, comfortably paid bachelorhood, so as to keep the sum of the family's wealth intact with a single male heir. Should he have girls, either the first or the handsomest in the lot, would be married with a dowry befitting a nobleman's daughter. Her groom would be selected carefully for any affluent match that would further trade for the family's wine production. As for any other remaining daughters, to the nunnery they would go.

Orso was the noble son of an impressively rich Venetian, a merchant. Being sent by his father to attend to matters on *terra firma*, Orso quickly become a master of trade. He was ambitious and an excellent negotiator, even able to secure an occasional bargain from the tight-fisted Severiano for superior casks of *vino*. He was invited to lodge and dine with the family on his visits and turned into an amiable guest after sampling the vineyard's gifts, increasing in charm while suspending boorish manners. And so, the stern patriarch of the estate set out to arrange a match between his firstborn daughter Lagia and the merchant's son; the connection would ensure that the family would profit off of their grapes as long as she lived.

After several extended visits, Severiano was

certain that he'd have a marriage contract between his house and that of Orso's father. Opportunities to push the youths together to inspire affection had been abundant. Unexpectedly however, the desire that had grown in Orso's eyes for Lagia, sharply turned toward Mirella. What did it matter to Severiano *which* daughter married well, so long as his house reaped the riches? He proposed a contract, which Orso's father accepted, leaving Lagia only one place to go; a nunnery.

Mirella knew that Lagia had fallen in love with Orso during that initial courtship; only, she couldn't allow her *own* fate to be enclosure with the nuns. Her father had had no hesitations revealing such a destiny to her once his intentions for Lagia had been made obvious. Mirella had fallen to her knees on that night, before his commanding, comfortless presence. He was sitting to table, stabbing at a piece of roasted meat on his plate as he advised her to prepare. These would be her last weeks of freedom. His cold eyes met hers as he bit off a charred, greasy cut from the tip of his dagger, causing her impassioned breaths to seize in her throat. Eating in silence, except to call to a servant to fetch him more wine, he'd had no reaction to her tears.

The entire household was aware that Severiano

had been mounting every pretty servant, and even those not so comely, as well as a great many village women, since becoming master over his inheritance. He was eventually made to marry, but bedded another even while the banquet flowers from his nuptial day with Paula were still in full bloom. He'd even had another the night his wife succumbed to her travail. It was certain his bastards were boundless. Mirella believed she'd spotted a few: a dirty, neglected village boy with her father's face, an overworked kitchen girl with oven burns on her arms and Severiano's gestures.

Though the thought of being shut up with the nuns for the rest of her life drowned her with panic, neither would she have wanted to be forced to take a husband like her father. A nunnery cell, or a prisoner in marriage? For noblewomen, fetters were found in every direction. As the clock ticked on and enclosure seemed imminent, Mirella grappled for a way to ensure her escape from the nunnery, and even from the shackles of a pernicious husband. Right before her was Orso. If she could make him love *her*, perhaps someday, she could even find contentment with him. At her sister's expense, Mirella did what she had to do.

As it was now, she hadn't heard from her husband in well over two months. His regular route on land first led him north to Treviso, where they owned an estate passed down from Orso's father. Though it retained a steward, the place required a master's attention at monthly intervals. Mirella and the girls annually traveled there to celebrate Twelfth Night and Epiphany, staying on until the end of January. They were delicious escapes, closer to the country surroundings that Mirella had grown up with and favored, away from the damp Venetian winter.

Next, Orso always headed east to Vicenza where there he retained a small city dwelling and invested in the local trade. After a week's stay he headed on to Padua, stopping along the way to visit vineyards and other men in trade, eventually reaching Mirella's family home, which now belonged to her brother Liborio. Orso had always hired loyal and hardworking men to follow behind each step of his trail, either to safely deliver or pick up those shipments he'd meant to move. He'd taken five men this time, all of which had made it to the estate in Padua. Orso however, had never arrived.

The men presumed that Orso had altered his plans and had returned to Venice at some point along the journey. They were the laborers in any case, and could retrieve these last barrels of wine under Liborio's direction. Mirella had written to her brother's wife Gostanza, and in the letter had inquired after her husband. The letter of reply came the very day that the hired men returned to Venice. They had not met with Orso on the ride back, and hadn't expected to, assuming he was already in *Venezia*. Gostanza's letter also contained a similar guess; that as Mirella cut open the seal of their correspondence, her goodly husband would have already been settled back at home.

Turning from worry, the missive relayed other news, such as her sister-in-law's pregnancy with her 11th child. Gostanza was always round and rosy; it was the country air, a bountiful table, and an ardent husband. In the letter, there was also the report of the death of a beloved servant of their house, a woman who had been Liborio, Lagia and Mirella's nursemaid, now more recently assigned to Gostanza's brood.

When Mirella was nine years old, this guardian strongly reprimanded her for something long forgotten, for which she'd certainly deserved the censure. Being impetuous and vengeful however, Mirella snuck juicy ripe grapes into the woman's bedchamber and carefully hid them one by one beneath the nurse's bedding. In the dark of night, with only the flicker of a few short candles, Mirella knew that the tired woman would fall upon the fruit, which would be ruinous to her bedclothes and nightgown. Though she knew she wouldn't be witness to the provoking event, she at the very least expected some sort of satisfying reaction from the woman the following morning. Whatever the consequences from her father, Mirella wanted to see the frustration on the woman's face.

The nurse was as cheerful as ever the following day and no scenes of furry took place. It was baffling. Hadn't the woman slept in her bed last night? Had another servant circumvented the plot and removed the grapes before the lady had made it to her rest? Mirella spent the day annoyed, but soon forgot it all for play, as children do. But as she went to bed that evening, easing beneath her warm coverlet, a cool creature slithered past her bare ankle. She screamed intensely and threw off the blanket just as a sizeable brown serpent slipped off the bed and undulated into a corner of the room. Servants came running at her screeching and the reptile was promptly dropped out of a window, a snake of the harmless variety. Mirella knew that no one would believe her if she blamed the gracious nursemaid, especially as lizards and serpents often made their way indoors and into close warm places, such as slippers or trunks full of linens. So she remained mute, and the both of them carried on as if nothing had happened. But as Mirella grew older, she developed a silent respect for the nurse, noting how well the woman negotiated around her onerous father and the general difficulties which women of their time, and servants all, faced. Mirella too, wanted to grow into a woman who could dance around danger.

Terribly frightening news came in Gostanza's letter as well, word of the plague east of Padua, not far from the route Orso and his men regularly traveled. Mirella shuddered. Though she had not been alive in 1528, the late nursemaid had and would share gruesome tales with her and her siblings. Lagia had always preferred enchanting stories, but Liborio and Mirella liked to be shocked and would beg to hear about the woman's memories of the scourge. Thousands, from Venice to Milan, had suffered and perished from the most horrible deaths. Even now, nearly 50 years later, churches were still being erected and candles lit in tribute to the lost, and in gratitude for the end of that blaze of pestilence. Prayers of deliverance were often uttered by those who'd survived; pleas that the curse would never return.

It had already returned, here and there like a

dangerous brushfire that would blessedly burn out before catching the forest. Strange that there was talk of it inland, as the plague often took hold in Venice first, brought from places exotic aboard merchant ships. Had a traveling merchant left out of Venice with death riding on his back, only to expire along the road? Some village fool would have rushed in to help the wealthy stranger, only to receive ruin rather than reward. But this was just speculation. Who was to know exactly where and how it had started. Perhaps it wasn't even the plague. False news was always circulating.

Folding the letter, Mirella sighed. While deaths, births and afflictions were taking place elsewhere, she had other pressing matters to consider. Her husband had not been seen by a single other person for at least a month. She would soon have to resign herself to the worst. Even in these last days, she'd kept a mountain of inquiries at bay; everyone wanted to know when Orso would return. But what if he didn't?

Mafalda

"**N**ot dead, sweet *signorina*?" The words were grossly breathy, as though the emaciated, greasy worm had just been darting up the steps of the *Ponte di Rialto*. His skeletal torso visibly heaved with some labor recently ceased. He was tall, dressed in tweedy rags covered in dark stains, blood. His head was shaved meanly, exposing scabby cuts, and his eyes were dark and beady. Even from where she sat, Mafalda could see fetid black teeth bucking out from his smirking mouth. The corpse bearer hungrily looked her over, as though she were a rabbit trapped in a snare, ready to be skewered. Though in a hellish place and situation, Mafalda was too aghast to focus on the fear. As she stared blankly at the man, those warnings about his kind came quickly to mind.

Monatti were summoned to homes to take away the corpses when plague crept up over any Italian city. The men employed were usually criminals. Often, they were so corrupt as to have been sentenced to death for rape or murder. But the plague brought desperation; who else would chance removing a stinking body covered in contagious boils but Venice's dregs, imprisoned in squalor and with nothing to lose?

31

Having before been slotted to die, they were now free to roam the city at will. Worse, they squeezed the coin from every family whether destitute or rich, threatening to leave the rotting, infectious bodies behind if their demands weren't met. Mafalda had heard horrifying examples of *monatti* purposefully exposing the local wells and walkways to pieces of blackened plague flesh, hoping that the families surrounding that *campo* would be struck down, bringing them more business. 'Ruthless evildoers' were not adequate words to describe them; they were *devils*. She had seen so herself when a local washing woman, a widow whose son had died in the first days of the plague to leave her completely alone, had met with one.

It was hardly a week into the first confirmations of death when Mafalda had witnessed the lady from her window, bickering through her tears with a *monatto*. Men were already being released from their dank cages to take up their grim positions, like an army of roaches flooding out from sordid dark corners. So too were they already taking advantage, though the scourge had just begun. The monster grabbed the woman by the hair and slammed her head into the stones at the face of her dwelling, crushing a cheekbone. The violence had certainly begun with a squabble over the fee to remove her dead son from her house, a sum she likely couldn't procure. Two brave men of the neighborhood ran to the skirmish from across the square and repeatedly jabbed the dog with their swords. Should it have been but a few days more into their city's plight, there would have been no rescue, as the dying would soon be found in every home, with neighborly love forsaken. The *monatto's* body was left on the stones for his brethren to take up. The injured lady was hysterical, later seen dragging her grown son out using the mere force of her grief; the two corpses waited side by side.

Though Mafalda didn't know it, the woman's efforts to remove her son from her house didn't save her from the curse. She was found at dawn two days later, sitting upright, ghoulish and bruised before her open door. Her head was titled to the sky with open eyes as though she had watched her last sunrise. Within the week, it was the same with those valiant rescuers, and many more besides. Where she sat, Mafalda's family flickered into her thoughts. How many of them still breathed? Perhaps none? Perhaps all. How could she know, from within this pit?

"Come sweet lady, I will help you out from there.

Come and take my hand and I will bring you someplace *safeeeee*." The last word was drenched in spittle and deceit. Mafalda already knew that should the snake pull her out, he'd force himself upon her in the light of day, then choke her and throw her dead back into the pit. What was she to do?

Her mind was so dull with cold that she was confused at once to hear *two* women, one at a groan and the other at a whisper. She looked to the outstretched, filthy hand of the *monatto* who was beckoning her to trample the dead and come to him. Her eyes then darted to a delicate hand peppered with dark splotches that leapt up to grab the *monatto*'s leg, weakly but urgently; the source of the moan was the reason he'd before been panting. A woman nearly dead of the plague lying there just out of sight; the *monatti* were known to throw as yet undead into the shallow pits. He was out of breath from dragging her. Evidently, this same error was how Mafalda had woken to find herself in the grave. Fiercely kicking the arm away, as if to a scampering rat to the ribs, he reached out further to Mafalda and attempted the most convincing face a deceiver could muster. The expression was revolting.

A woman's whisper, the second feminine uttering,

came from just beyond Mafalda's toes. Looking down past the length of her thin, colorless legs, she again saw those barren eyes of the dead woman, yet the lashes appeared to *flutter* and there was a blink. Apart from the purple round around her blackened eye, her skin was so pale as to be marble. She *must* be dead...she *was* dead. And yet, she spoke, her lips moving slowly as she stared directly into Mafalda's eyes. Her mouth formed into a faint smile as the murmur came, "At *your* neck a pearl, at *mine* a blade."

Instantly the eyes grew still again, as they had been before. Though Mafalda had yet to move her toes even once, blue and lifeless as they were, with the pain she knew would come, she worked her mind to curl her toes down and lifted up her frame just so to gaze over them. Agony ripped through her shins. There at the neck of the dead woman was indeed, a dagger's tip pointing out of the snow. It was rusted and toothy. Surely the humble tool of one of the fallen, broken off of a belt or even hurled into the pit, found useless by one of the thieving gravediggers. The cruder the better, she thought.

Noemi

Noemi knew that poetic love was a ridiculous thing; those narratives in which youths found themselves enamored and at odds with their steely parents, ultimately and consequently severed from their desires. These tales were meant to be captivating; they encouraged the hearts of young ladies to soar and ache, alleviated their boredom, and caught them up in imaginary tangles. Noemi knew those wistful stories were not reality however. No, true love was far more beautiful than a tale; the words for it were beyond invention. It could only be known through experience.

Noemi and her sisters had always experienced some relaxed freedoms while growing up in Venice. But unless it was the *Carnevale* or another sanctioned affair and all four of them were appropriately masked and sharing a family gondola, they were rarely permitted to go out at night. This was just one durable rule applied to all noble daughters for their protection. Orso, being very wealthy, was certain to permit one or even two of his daughters to marry with a dowry befitting their rank. Noemi had her eye on a certain man. He was a craftsman, a woodworker, a maker of gondolas. But even if Noemi was one of the chosen to become a bride, she'd never have been permitted to take Ilario for her husband, no matter how esteemed his trade was in Venice. She hadn't told anyone of her secret fervor, not even her sisters.

She'd passed his workshop so often on her way to say prayers at her family's church, the *Santa Maria dei Miracoli*. He was a man she'd espied many times over the years. However, she'd never considered his person until just one year before. On that first morning, when her eyes were opened, she'd inexplicably paused to fully regard the woodworker as he carved the fittings for a fine new vessel. He stood out to her, working in the open air just before his door. At once she recognized him as tenacious, yet tender while he worked. A steadfast, patient man. Anyone who made gondolas for a living would need those qualities, for a single boat could take months to finish. She instantly admired him, to say nothing of how enticing she found his form. She wanted to know him, to learn of his other qualities. She'd been seduced on sight.

After that day, Mirella must have found her daughter's religiosity fervently sparked, the girl strangely devout. On those outings, Noemi always went veiled and passed slowly before his residence. Longing began to temper her naturally brisk steps. But prayer wasn't the only excuse she used to leverage a leave from the *palazzo*. She'd often offer herself when her mother mentioned a need from the market stalls, despite these jogs being a task for a servant. Mirella had been raised with ample freedom in the countryside and didn't keep as strict reins on her girls as other noble matriarchs did with theirs; she always let her go. Noemi also excused herself to visit friends or would make a show of taking charitable baskets of scraps to the almshouses.

His dwelling was across from a thin *calle* she walked, with a slim canal flowing between them. He was older than her, perhaps by 10 years, maybe more. The two-story wooden building contained a workshop on the first floor, where the windows were often thrown open so that the sunlight could flood in. The apartment above was where Noemi assumed he lived. He could often be seen working a piece of lumber upon a weathered table before the workshop, wood shavings scattered around his feet. She could smell the oils released from the tree slabs as he carved, even from across the water. Once, the fragrance was certainly that from a fir tree and she instantly lusted that his calloused, sap-sticky hands were reaching under her skirts as she inhaled that sharp fresh scent from right off of his skin. She was surprised by her wild imaginings, but every time she smelled pine after that, she thought of him. She even secured some small linen sachets and filled them with heady pine needles and dried juniper berries, placing them under her bed pillow and between her delicately folded linens for their scent.

The winter holiday spent with her mother and sisters in Treviso that year ran over with yearnings for Ilario. The magical boughs of fir and the amorous red color of berries, the sips of sweet wine, the juicy oranges that one of the keepers grew indoors, the spices and merry laughter, the oysters delivered to them still plump and thriving from the cold sea. All of these things stirred her senses and she dreamt what it would be like to enjoy such pleasures with a man. What was it like to have a husband, to possess a lover, especially one so fine as Ilario? No longer restricted to the canals and bridges of the lagoon, she ran through fields of snow with her sisters and the cheeks of all were daily blushed and healthy. Their temporary freedom gave Noemi a false hope; that a happy fate would triumph, and that she could circumvent any bleak marriage plans her parents might be considering for her even now. She wanted to believe that *each* of her sisters would find happiness. And though she had yet to face Ilario in the flesh, glimpses had convinced her that she could love him. If only there was a way to meet him. Such an improbable hope came true, for one day she did.

Noemi had been gifted with a small and smooth wooden plank with rounds carved out, which nested hardened colors in them. She'd always loved to stand before a painting, to admire an artist's work, her red curls cascading as she stretched her neck from side to side, taking in small details. Canvases were otherworldly, heroic and arousing. Knowing her inclination for art, Fina had given her this set of paints on the 17th anniversary of her birth. One morning, Noemi sat waterside of the *palazzo* to use them. She began by sketching the Byzantine windows of the palatial residence across from their own. Later she would paint over the drawing. It was a relatively quiet canal, especially so early (with the exception of the occasional squawking seabird). And though she frowned at her initial attempts to draw even those simple combinations of basic shapes which made up the casements, she very much enjoyed the task. Studiously concentrating on her sketch, which lay upon a board over her lap, she gasped when looking up to her scene once more. Before her floating in a polished gondola, stood the man she'd embraced in her dreams. She sat erect while her cheeks reflexively bloomed; one hand clenched dark chalk while the other pressed her drawing firmly down upon her lap.

He wished her a *bongiorno* with a fluid Venetian tongue, and asked her if this was indeed the House of Orso. Many who lived in *Venezia* had not been born there; it was a diverse city filled with exotic languages, and even Italian dialects varied greatly. But this man had come from a line of Venetians, she was certain. She wondered how long the men in his lineage had made boats. Perhaps it was even from the birth of this city from out of the waters.

She nodded, bewildered. In silence, cocking her copper head and furrowing her pretty brow, she watched him stow his single oar and tie up to one of several mooring poles hedging the marble stairs leading up to the stone platform where she sat. After mounting the steps, he cautiously approached and paused before her. First bowing, he then offered her a warm smile. Once standing tall again, Noemi quite dazed, he stated his business.

"I am Ilario. I have received a commission from the House of Orso. Am I to guess that you are a daughter to Orso, my lady?" His eyes were steady and kind.

Why was her father in need of a new vessel? Hadn't they enough gondolas? Perhaps it was some political bribe or wedding gift. Did she care? It was hard to think clearly.

A nervous pressure in her chest, she slowly nodded and said, "He is within, good sir. I shall find him for you. I shall go in with you."

As awkward as the choppy words may have been, Ilario smiled even more warmly, as if pleased. Creases grew in the tanned skin around his handsome eyes. Trying withal to be graceful, she calmly stood and gently placed her items on her seat, careful not to wipe her chalky fingers over her dress, and set out before him into the *palazzo*.

After Ilario was in the presence of her father and discussing the new order, Noemi stood breathless without the door of her father's meeting chamber. Ilario had brushed past her as he crossed into the room and she'd smelled him, wood smoke and cinnamon. The man could afford a pinch of exotic spices; fortune must have touched his calloused hands. He'd been mannerly and confident, so attractive before her that she'd feared she'd trip on her own feet as she guided him into the inner quarters. Her heart now leapt, bounding beneath her bodice. Perhaps this little turn of fate would afford her some further glimpses of this man up-close. He would certainly visit again; such commissions took time. Perhaps they would even speak again, more than just those few words like today. The anticipation drove a flood of want into her bosom. She leaned her hot forehead upon the imposing wooden door to cool it and closed her eyes for a moment. When she opened them, her eyes facing downwards, she chanced to spy the point of one of her embroidered slippers sneaking past the hem of her gown. Beside it she saw a small and deeply purple, almost black, orb attached to a green leaf. Stooping, she found that it was a berry. What kind of berry? She sniffed it, but it was unfamiliar to her.

Walking languidly toward the palace kitchen she sought out Martinella, hearth keeper and second mother, and asked her what it was. The cook eyed it curiously, her old and crinkled face filled with lines and her soft cheeks pink from working before the flames since before sunrise. Looking up to Noemi, she answered her question with a question. Where'd she find this diabolical fruit? Such as it was, a lethal assassin berry from the deadly nightshade plant!

Paola

The servant girl's screaming sounded muffled as Paola fell to the cold stone floor. She had just been speaking to Tonia and Martinella in the hall about a precious strand of soft pink pearls hung at intervals along a linked chain of gold. The necklace had been a gift from her father on Twelfth Night, received when they'd last so merrily stayed in Treviso. Paola was a particular sort of person who liked everything in its place. Lately, a few things had gone missing.

There was a beloved feather quill. She'd purchased it from a merchant in *Piazza San Marco*. The feather itself was from the tail of a Chinese Golden Pheasant. The rachis that ran down the middle of the plume was of a turquois blue, the afterfeathers a piercing red and the vane, a pattern of yellow and black dispersed in odd swirls. She'd always loved to see the birds, though sadly caged, that came from off of the merchants' ships. Those vessels carried a great many precious things from Persia, Egypt and China. And though she never saw a live Golden Pheasant, this merchant claimed to have trapped and feasted upon one in the mountains of China, far to the east. It greatly amused Paola to hear the bird described as best as it could be remembered. It was a rainbow colored creature, far more beautiful than the dull-feathered pheasant she'd seen running the fields on *terra firma*. He'd kept some of its feathers, selling Paola one from the bird's long tail. She loved to write letters with the quill and ponder discovering animals in distant lands, places she didn't ever expect see. That was unless a pirate kidnapped her. This could happen of course, she lived in Venice on the Adriatic Sea. That's why there was the *Festa delle Marie*, an annual celebration for the return of 12 maidens kidnapped by pirates centuries before. There had been others too, it could happen to her. She wished it would; Paola wanted to see the world for herself.

She was also missing a vial of perfume; an essence of green apples that she relished. The perfume seller had acquired it in Florence; pure and cutting, unmistakably *pomo*. The bottle that contained it was made of pearly blown glass, and the liquid was stopped from running out with a tiny cork. In the sides of the vial's lip, there were two little holes so that the bottle could be hung from a chain. If ever she would run out of the precious oil, and she was certain to, she could take it back to fill again, and could wear it around her neck like an ornament. Since she'd acquired it, it had always hung down aside her chamber mirror.

She'd also had a few less valuable items disappear. Orso often forwarded on special little gifts to his wife and daughters when he was away. Among other things within a small trunk that Mirella had lately received, was a linen sack filled with hard confections fashioned like miniature lemons and dusted with sugar. These favors had arrived at the *palazzo* not long after he'd last been seen. As her mother knew of her proclivity toward tart fruit, she'd given them to Paola. The wooden dish she displayed them in recently seemed to have less than what she'd eaten. And, a pair of fine slippers embroidered with blue Cyanus flowers from Croatia had also danced away, but not on *her* feet.

And then of course, there was the beloved necklace strung with rosy pearls. With three sisters, it didn't seem unnatural that they might borrow a trinket and forget to mention it to Paola. Yet, that had been very infrequent up until now. It had been the very opposite in fact. All older, it was *they* who doted on her by lending her their belongings. They rarely borrowed anything from Paola's chamber for themselves. So who was pilfering her treasures?

When she came to, she was sprawled on the floor with what felt like the entire household around her.

Tonia stood screeching like a distressed goose, which sent shocks through Paola's brain. There were also two of her father's hired men, who had likely come by the *palazzo* to seek out any news of Orso. They must have come running from the shrieking, soon to stand confused along the wall with their caps in their hands. They'd hurried toward action only to find a fainted daughter of the house, and were now posed awkwardly aside. Martinella, as arthritic as she was, slowly kneeled and hovered close over her. The old woman softly touched one of her eyelids and Paola groaned. Mirella and Fina stood loftily above, breathless from wherever they'd hailed. Her mother swiftly turned on Tonia, angry as a rabid dog, and slapped the girl hard. The young maid stood stunned and motionless as a pink mark started to develop on her cheek. Large tears began to tumble down her face and she whimpered.

"What are you *screaming* for, you *stupid* girl?" Barked Mirella.

Though hardly able to register it, Paola found her mother oddly harsh toward the servant. How vexed she was, her form rigid, her hands fisted at her sides. Tonia stuttered as she forced out the words.

"*Plague...madam*, it might be the *plague*. A missive from my cousin in Vicenza...she works in the House of

Prudenzio. Martinella read me the letter, as I can't make out words myself. It's in the villages, madam. We *all* could perish." The tears were copious now.

Mirella's eyes widened as Tonia began to weep nervously into her hands. So it was spreading. Martinella stretched out a wrinkled, delicate hand into the air. One of the aimless men bumbled to her side to help her up from her difficult position. As she stood, brushing at her skirts, she addressed the lady of the house.

"This is no plague m'lady. I've seen *that* devil run through a house." The old woman paused and made the sign of the cross over herself. "Your youngest has been stricken. Do you see her pupils, as large and black as ripe grapes?" Martinella scrunched her wiry brows together until they looked like one line. "The lady Noemi found a death cherry just before m'lord left for Treviso, *in* the house. I cast it into the lagoon. I imagine more found their way in through the door? We best put her to bed madam, and *see* if she wakes in the morning."

Mirella motioned to the second man, who immediately swooped in and picked up the invalid with ease, as if she were but a piece of parchment. Paola clasped her arms around his thick neck and rested her head upon his brawny shoulder, her black hair flowing over it. *So this is what it feels like to sway high atop a cypress tree* she thought, all lucidity falling away. How little she knew of trees; Venice hadn't many to climb, not that she'd have been permitted to scale one if there were. She'd normally have been mortified to be in the arms of a strange man, the arms of *any* man, yet this was comforting. But then, as if with a small dagger, the poison sharply slashed in her stomach and she cried out into the ruffled collar of the stranger's cotton shirt. She'd never felt a pain like that before. The man held her closer as he gingerly carried her down the hall. Too agonized to push off the onset of another faint, the last thing she remembered was the smell of leather and hay, the balm of the stranger's doublet.

Mafalda

Mafalda stared directly into the eyes of her would-be murderer from but inches away from his awestruck features. Her stare was feral and her strength incomprehensible for her weakened condition. She was not afraid; an embrace with death had made her wild. A strange, untimely serenade suddenly floated through her head as she sneered at her foe, the words stringing along like a rope between mooring pole and vessel.

Gone and lost my precious pearl?

Hast thou passed out through my door?

I shall not live if you're not with me.

Boatman, boatman, swiftly.

Bring her back, and quickly.

Bring her back...

My breaking heart to speed thyne oar...

She couldn't remember from what minstrel she'd heard the song, or within which palace, nor understood why it came to mind in this moment. The past was hazy. Hot blood seared her frozen fisted hand, still yet clinging to the jagged weapon. The foul, simpering wretch crumpled and fell down before her feet, clutching his guts. His eyes grew larger and larger with terror as vermilion began to bubble up in his throat. He coughed and sputtered; specks and globs of blood spattering his filthy ragged chest. The woman who had tugged at his ankle lay expired beside him, blackened buboes exposed at her neck. The gentle lady had met an excruciating end. Soon, the mongrel *monatto* who would have buried both women alive, would meet a hellish end too, only it would be eternal.

Mafalda had already met with death, yet had lived. That outcome however was not assured. A rush of blood presently numbed the cold, and drove her movements forward, but it wouldn't last. Even as she leaned down, lightening flashed in her spine while she sliced a ribbon strained over the dead woman's chest. Gently, she rolled the still supple corpse out of its cloak and pulled the filched mantle up over her own shoulders. An infectious stink wafted around her as she whipped the hood up over her head, accidently smearing coagulating blood from her messy hand onto one cheek while clumsily avoiding the point of her own knife. The smells of metal and sickness made Mafalda gag and teeter with faintness. She worked to inhale wintery breaths at a slow pace to ward off her urge to lie down while scanning the field.

She was on a small island, one of Venice's

quarantine islands certainly. These were usually used as a temporary residence for merchants, where such wayfarers would abide for 40 days after sailing into the lagoon, ensuring their men and imported wares showed no signs of harboring pestilence. Only then were they admitted into the city. Mafalda had been boated over while unconscious. It was clear that she was at the far tip of the isle, her burial pit not some twenty yards off from the water's edge and perhaps just freshly dug. Before her spanned a good distance of unspoiled land covered in a light layer of snow, a few muddy footprints tracking over it. Just past this, a meadow of death. Cavernous pits, visibly filled, even from where she stood. Spiderlike *beccamorti* scurried and dug and threw in bodies. Smoke drifted from piles of burning brush, which kept the hands of the gravediggers thawed. Spying several far larger and raging bonfires, she could only hope that it was just wood fueling the flames. That was not the direction to walk in. It would be preferable to stumble over into the frigid waters and drown herself.

She avoided a glimpse into her own grave, from which escape was only managed by crawling pitifully over the dead, and which also entailed placing one free and fragile hand into the claws of a predator so that she could be pulled out. The price of getting out forced her to commit a mortal sin, but it was necessary; she wouldn't have survived a single moment of violent handling. She scanned the perimeter of the water's edge as the sun in the sky began to dim. Soft grey clouds were drifting in, working to filter out the sun's sharp light overhead; snowflakes began to fall. Mafalda closed her eyes and uttered a prayer for deliverance. When she opened them again, she sharply cackled the laugh of the insane; did God answer desperate pleas so swiftly?

Moving stiffly and unnaturally, she began to shuffle toward the dying *monatto's* boat bobbing at the water's edge, freshly moored. She hadn't spotted it before. She counted the outlines of the newest arrivals. Two stiff and prostrate bodies on the sandy bank, and one yet in the boat. Inside the vessel was a woman with coiled red tresses, laying facedown. Though she could have been a courtesan with such a fine gown, it was more likely a noble lady. The figure was slim and youthful. Mafalda hesitated to move any further. Were not those curls and form so strikingly comparable to a beloved sister's?

Tonia

There was nothing more terrifying to Tonia than the plague, and her worst reminder of it was a painting displayed in her mistresses' church. There were so many fine churches in Venice, unlike the small countryside house of worship that she grew up attending near Padova, where no art was to be found at all. This painting, she supposed, sat in sight of everyone to remind the flock of their fragility and sinful natures, so that they would be diligent to live devout lives and avoid falling into the traps of temptation. She often had to accompany the ladies of Orso's house on their errands, and it sometimes fell to her to carry a basket for Noemi when she went to say prayers, which seemed to be *all* of the time anymore. It irritated her that Noemi walked so slowly along the way and back home again, for Tonia had much work to do. Especially when Noemi only spent a few minutes lighting a candle and bending her head under the cross. Why didn't she just stay home to say her prayers if she was only going to spend such short a time at her devotions?

While she waited for Noemi to complete her worship, and not inclined to sit to prayers so often herself, she'd amble before expressive marble statues or gaze at the intricately carved, decorative wooden ceiling. But propped upon a sturdy-legged stand, in a shadowy back corner of the echoing house, was the piece that moved her to terror. The painting exhibited a terrible plague that had befallen a village. It was the Black Death. People, pale-green and emaciated, smothered the canvas, as skeletons danced on their heads or pushed spears through their bodies or ran over them while riding skeleton horses. Nobles and peasants alike, the people together fell into heaps while devils danced around bonfires and skeletal birds picked at their eyeballs. It made her shudder every time she saw it and was painted just after the most recent scourge. She wondered if Martinella had beheld such a scene? The old woman was always making the sign of the cross over herself whenever a single word of the plague was mentioned. Tonia's grandmother had told her horrible stories as well, which were far better forgotten than shared. She wished she'd never heard them at all. The last time she'd viewed that painting, Noemi snuck up behind her and sounded a little roar to frighten her; how it *did*. She'd jumped and nearly expelled the contents of the lady's basket. Those sisters were always teasing and having a laugh, Tonia thought they were all spoiled. *Especially* Paola.

So as to protect the innocence of the youngest, Mirella always sent Tonia (who was two years older), with Paola on outings to the market or on visits if one of her older sisters wasn't accompanying her. She was a frail thing. Tonia wished she'd eat more meat and stop acting so irritatingly delicate. She herself was an able-bodied worker and proud of it. Paola certainly wouldn't have been able to scrub a *palazzo* floor or chop up a reluctant log to keep a fire going. Tonia thought she was dull and that she too often played upon her slightness and innocence to gain attention.

There was one thing however that *really* put a match under her skirts. Paola always had these cravings for fruit, seemingly revolted by heartier vegetables, such as the plain root vegetables that Tonia was raised on. Such fine tastes were given in to and so, Paola was frequently given permission to float off to the fruit vendors, with Tonia as the escort in tow. Tonia absolutely hated the way the girl, with her pale skin, dark hair and large round eyes, always looked like a dazed doe weaving through a magical realm the moment she began walking through the market displays. She became enchanted by each piece of exotic fruit that the merchants weekly brought, and would look up at the men with wonder every time they cut a rare slice and offered it to her. They never offered Tonia a piece, for she was but a noble girl's servant. And even with all those enticing flavors, Paola still went back again and again for those simple, sour apples. She herself couldn't bide the taste of them, even if they did smell pretty.

There was something even more to her distaste. Tonia had met a young man on an errand alone to pick up a sack of white cornmeal for Martinella. Just her age, he'd rushed right into her in the market, hurrying to somewhere. She nearly lost her grip on the meal, which would have gotten her a terrible scolding from the tired hearth master. He'd had a handsome smile, unkempt brown hair and soft green eyes. He'd caught her balance by manhandling her arms to help her get upright. Even after he released his grip, she'd felt the firmness of his hold and momentarily lost speech from the power of such an instant attraction. They spoke for a few minutes, introducing themselves to one another. His father was a farmer on *terra firma* and they boated over twice weekly to sell their bounty. He'd made a few jokes about his clumsiness and begged her forgiveness, which she gave willingly. Excitement had clutched her like a hawk's talons upon a supple field rabbit.

Too soon, he continued on his way. After that, she hadn't minded so much following after that annoying child to the market, for she hoped to seek out her acquaintance and create an opportunity to speak to him again. She wouldn't mind marrying a farmer of the Veneto. She'd stop being *just* a servant and would manage a cottage all her own. And for such a goodly husband, Tonia would gladly birth a brood of plump and healthy babies, all who would appreciate vegetables. Even though they had only met once, she daydreamed about him. She wondered whether he farmed grapes in a vineyard, or cherries in an orchard, or perhaps pumpkins in the field. How she loved pumpkin soup. She'd make it for him, and wouldn't he love her for it!

One soft sunny morning, she saw him again. Only, he was discovered to be the *apple* farmer's son and Tonia was following behind Paola. Though he politely acknowledged her, it was immediately evident that on his meeting the imp, he preferred *her*. Of course he did, with her slim waist and silky dress and raven locks and delicate slippers and her inexhaustible *lust* for apples. She hated him after that, even if it wasn't his fault that he was attracted to that morning's chatty, shiny starling. It was just that it had ruined her delicate hopes, a brittle dream that pleasantly took her away from scrubbing marble floors, washing countless dishes, and however noble the producers, emptying stinking chamber pots. She'd slinked off to find the medicinal plants; Martinella had been complaining about an obstinate cut on her hand that wouldn't heal. She'd work to distract herself by finding something for it.

Paola remained behind to wonder over the apple varieties while the farmer's boy sliced up a few for her to sample. It was improbable that if Tonia had still been present, any would have been offered to her.

Mirella

Rereading the immaculate script, it was hard to comprehend the finality of the words. Another letter, bearing terrible news. Sound no longer entered her ears, as if she were buried in some silent catacomb. The letter had arrived from Padua that very morning, informing her that her sister Lagia had succumb to the plague. She had been the first of a handful to perish. Two evenings before the one on which she'd died, she'd been assigned to retrieve the alms passed through a discrete turntable at the street-side door of the convent. It was later concluded that charitable items within the collection were to blame for passing on the disease that took her life; donations innocently left by well-meaning strangers who at the time, may not have even known that they themselves were sick. A small trunk was to follow this sorrowful information, some few religious items that Lagia had cherished, but only after its contents had sufficiently aired from without her tainted cell. The letter was signed in the name of the convent, leaving no particular nun to credit, though Mirella knew it was usually the abbess who tended to such matters, if she hadn't been one of the casualties.

Decades had passed since they'd parted and this was the first missive to ever arrive from that dungeon, which was her sister's permanent home. It wouldn't have been surprising if Lagia had never forgiven Mirella for stealing the future that had rightfully belonged to her. In confinement, how she must have grieved the loss of her freedom. Mirella had never sent word to Lagia at the convent either. What could she have written that wouldn't have pained her sister further? Severiano hadn't been the sort of father to maintain familial affections; it was unlikely he'd ever picked up his quill for his daughter. Liborio tried, but according to his wife Gostanza, each inquiry into their sister's life had been sent back unopened and he eventually ceased altogether.

Mirella carefully refolded the paper until the severed halves of sealing wax met, appearing as if the letter had never been opened. Somberly, she walked over to the crackling fire that kept her chamber in a cocoon of warmth, and dropped it upon the flickering flames. What good would it do to keep it, to read it ever again? She couldn't make amends now and further, had long ago pushed away what sentiments remained in her heart. She might come to grieve the news more fully, but more than anything, the report had been unexpected and frightening.

Mirella reached for a glass decanter and poured a goblet full of heady drink, a yield from one of Orso's best vintners, and sat down before the fire. To a rapping at her door, she cried out to be left alone, whoever it may be. Footsteps nervously shuffled away from her chamber as she took a sip of wine.

"Where are you now, my lusty husband?" She whispered into the heat.

The hint of a smirk moved upon her beautiful lips. Even without a similar letter to officiate *his* death, she was certain he was as far away as Lagia. With as many weeks as had passed, it was now time that she arranged for her daughters and the servants to don more sober attire; they too ought to accept what she already knew. This also meant that the girls would need to begin readying themselves for a change. Reining in their naturally oblivious, spoiled and merry living, while concentrating harder on their devotions, seemed appropriate. They were all of age, women now, even 15-year-old Paola. It was time, though the transitions wouldn't be easy. Upheavals never were. Mirella's faint grin quickly disappeared, her looks soon stony as the hearth's shadows danced throughout the room.

Plans for Noemi were a little different than for the

rest. Her nuptial vows would be ironic considering Noemi had lately shown more piety than all of her other sisters combined. As she mentally reviewed the union she was contriving, Mirella remembered just how matrimony had fallen into her own lap.

Remo had taught her a great many things. He was four years older and was the son of her father's steward. Though of a respected family, he was not her equal. It was he that had taught her to taste the dirt for its properties, to see if it would accept the vine. She'd also tasted the dust when they'd rolled together over the earth. It had happened a great many times, hidden away in the vineyard, coupling together like two feral animals in spring, covered in sweat, soil and dew. They'd lay naked on hot summer nights and rejuvenate off the sweet grapes. Once after such copulations and nearly re-dressed, only attending to the last ties of their garments, Lagia had come upon them. She'd been looking for Mirella, for there had been a special arrival at dusk. Orso had just roared into the estate once again, and his affections had been tenderly fixed on Lagia. Cheerful with anticipation, she wished to gossip with her sister about her intended union with such a platitudinous noble. The house was currently preparing for a late banquet for the family and all of the men in Orso's party.

When Lagia saw them, she discreetly turned away without a word and made her way back to the villa. Mirella soon followed behind, but did not seek out her sister before preparing alone in her chamber for what a handmaiden had informed her, was likely to be a long night. She quickly bathed away her assignation. But after finding herself dressed, perfumed and adorned, she became unexpectedly nauseous and vomited into her chamber pot.

Having learned enough with Remo to know how to seduce a man, she quickly found herself married with Orso. Pregnant or not, and regardless that Lagia had the right to the man, she couldn't allow herself to be sent to a nunnery. She'd have gone senseless within weeks of being cloistered. Even if she had been willing to accept that destiny, once her condition was found out, the nuns would have punished and shunned her; her baby dispatched to be raised by strangers. That was *if* her father didn't drag her out first and crack her head open upon the steps of the convent in sight of her religious sisters; Severiano was capable of that, she was certain.

After the vows had taken place, Orso rode onward to Venice to prepare for the arrival of his new wife.

Accompanied for her protection by two of his trusted men, and for her comfort one of her family's handmaidens, on horseback all, Mirella rode toward her destiny. The roads were extreme. Halfway from Padua to the sea she began to experience a subtle piercing, and then an immense cramping. She'd stopped the party to exact her privy in a dense span of brush, first distracting her companions with the pleasantest orders to eat and take their rest.

Believing she had only to empty her bowel, neither the handmaiden nor any other living was the wiser when Mirella lost her and Remo's imperceptible miracle within a clot of blood. She could hardly be sure herself, only confirmed when her body never grew with child and her interval bleeding returned. Blessedly, the remaining distance of the journey was less harsh, for she was riding pale and with continual faintness. The maid only guessed that it was the fatigue of an abrupt wedding combined with a strenuous journey. Mirella was eventually delivered into the vessel of a boatman hired by Orso, who was moored and waiting patiently at the edge of the lagoon. Rowing out toward the Adriatic, it was not long before they were floating through the canals of one of the most illustrious cities in Europe.

Noemi

The poison berry was odd, but all sorts of vendors and visitors entered their home to meet with either one of her parents. Perhaps it was a dye maker or a physician practiced in making tinctures that came up a berry short as they exited the *palazzo*. Martinella carried it out of sight and it was forgotten. A few days later, Orso left on his routine trip upon *terra firma*. Despite his constant gruffness, Noemi was fond of her father and believed the house had less spirit when he was away. And though his frequent departures usually didn't elicit much feeling, this time, she felt strangely sorry that she hadn't wished him Godspeed and good health the morning he'd left.

She soon shook off the sentiment, becoming more and more drawn to her daydreaming of Ilario. Along with her frequent secret walks past his workhouse, she began practicing her painting on the stone dock of the waterside entrance more often; especially during the hours tradesmen were more likely to visit. Should the gondola maker come again, she would easily miss the occasion if she were to be in any other part of the home. Noemi quickly gave up on her forced preparatory sketches, and instead, joyfully swished indiscriminate strokes of watercolor. Some days it was a spread of turquoise and white inspired by the sky. On others, it was a canvas full of green-blue streaks from the flow of the canal before her. There were also the swirls of black or red or brown, mimicking the lustrous lacquers of boats. And then, on one afternoon as clouds grew overhead and a cool wind blew in, she looked up from a canvas covered in violet stain to see him slowing his boat before her. His irresistible smile would have brought her to her knees if she had been standing. He called out to her.

"Noble mistress, will you not deliver a parcel to lay wait for your good father and save me the trip within to give it to your mother in his stead? They are the plans for his gondola. I will not tarry, if you could but deliver them to the master's table." Though plainly a confident man, there was in his looks, a touch of nervousness.

To walk directly up to him, or to any man, like two strangers meeting on the street, lacked discretion. Of course, her mother had been soft about the girls and their freedoms. Most noble ladies were rarely allowed out onto the *calli* before they were wed, and certainly would never have gone unveiled or without a mask. Though Mirella did expect her daughters to have a companion along on their outings, she'd cared little whether they were disguised when walking to the market by light of day. To church, or out in the evening, were different matters. However, regardless of her looseness on the matter, Mirella might have something to say about Noemi approaching the tradesman at his boat for all of the neighbors to see.

She gazed up and around at all the windows in the *palazzo* across the water and then back and above to her own dwelling. There was no one watching, as far as she could see. The wind blew harder and a far distant booming could be heard, thunder. Looking back to Ilario, she felt entranced by the warmth she found in his face as the gust swayed him in his boat. What would it be like to lay her cheek against his? What would it sound like, listening to amorous whispers lilting from his lips? She blinked away her runaway thoughts and stood, gingerly setting the paintbrush and colors upon her seat.

The wind stirred up red curls that had come loose of a feminine plait pinned up from her neck, while the soft fabric of her long gown swished against bare ankles on approach to the edge of the marble dock. She wondered what her own expressions announced to him. Dazed and dull? Sensual? Stern? Coming to stand above him, she smiled softly yet silently, unable to think of anything to say. Slowly bending down and out towards him, she reached her hand for the renderings. He quickly slid his own hand between the leather doublet and chemise at his chest and produced a thick square of folded parchment, sealed with yellow wax. After handing it to her, she motioned to stand upright. It was best to retreat quickly from the boat so as not to appear as having a waterside meeting.

"Wait, mistress. Sweet lady, this is for *you*." The maker of gondolas called out in a low voice with a searching look on his face and reached into his doublet once more. On impulse, her eyes grew wide and she arched an eyebrow. What was this? Had her ears deceived her? "Please take this letter. It is for your eyes alone."

Her hand quivered as it darted out to snatch the missive. The proper thing would have been to reject the offering. This had hardly been clandestine, anyone could see. But she didn't care; she'd have this letter. And now that it was in her hands, even without knowing the words that it contained, she'd have waggled a dagger before anyone who might try to take it away from her.

Firmly pressing his fingers to his lips, he waved them toward her, a silent kiss to bid her farewell.

Stunned, she watched as Ilario pushed off from the edge of the dock and began to oar his sleek vessel away from her. Soon out of sight, she thrust the correspondence, a small folded paper stamped with a red wax seal, down between her bodice and bosom. It burned into her breast; the anticipation was unbearable. As the first drops of rain began she hurried to snatch up her small canvas and supplies, some of heaven's tears altering the colors of her artwork, making diluted streaks. She thought the painting better for it. It would be her favorite piece.

Mafalda

Every Venetian woman who could afford to, and certainly every noblewoman, wore pearls. Some elaborate ladies dripped with them, hanging from the parts in their hair, creamy orbs dangling from their ears, stitched along the low necklines of their bodices, dotting the cuffs of their sleeves, pendulous on long necklaces. And to those brides-to-be, chokers and strands of lustrous pearls were given and worn. It was easy to pick out a newlywed, circlets of the precious adornments usually clung to her throat.

She'd learned from Noemi that their father had commissioned a new gondola. This was an unusual investment. Why did he need an additional boat when a cluster of fine vessels were already his, moored and bobbing beneath their *palazzo*? Her sister had seemed strangely animated when speaking about this boat, asking random questions directed to no one in particular, such as how long it would take a craftsman to complete this gondola and what variety of wood was most often used in one's construction. Mafalda could only guess while being amused by Noemi's excitement: pine, oak and walnut? She found Noemi's behavior changed, with her frequent trips to the church, dazed meanderings through the halls, and random interests. However, Fina was behaving even more oddly.

It had become a trend very commonly seen, a lady dyeing her hair blond in Venice. However, it tended to be more popular with the courtesans. There were a great many recipes for it, all odious concoctions. Some worked and some didn't, many made a woman's hair fall out. Some burned the scalp and left scars, while others used only harmless and common herbs. One important key however, was to sit out on the roof as often as possible during the height of the day, harnessing the sun's bleaching effects. It was a common thing for sunning ladies to wear large, spherical straw hats with a hole at the pinnacle, which allowed locks to spill out and be exposed without tanning delicate faces and necks. The women of Orso's house had thus far circumvented the movement, nurturing their natural shades. And though it wasn't wholly bizarre that Fina would decide to turn her brown tresses into the coveted blond, she'd become unnaturally occupied with working out different formulas to find just the right one. She was currently spending an inordinate amount of time perched on the garden terrace.

Mafalda had noted too how Fina was working to

perfect the twist and height of a coned hairstyle, so often seen on noblewomen and courtesans alike. All the ladies of their house had tried fashioning their hair in this way, but why was Fina so concerned with its design? Why had she so suddenly become vain?

Recently entering her chamber, Mafalda found Fina sitting before her mirror. She'd cheerily greeted her without receiving a response. Approaching from behind, her sister appeared to be in a stupor, her head hung low. Calling out again more directly, Fina's head sprung up and Mafalda could see in the reflection staring back at her, glisteningly damp skin, large black pupils and flushed cheeks. Fina quickly looked away from the mirror, and sharply stated that she was tired and wanted to be alone. Glancing at her table, Mafalda noted that it was becoming overrun with porcelain containers of makeup, vials of perfume, pots of dye and other indiscernible compounds. She particularly noticed an odd glass phial. Corked atop, within was a dark yet transparent liquid, purplish-black in color. It might have contained fragrance, yet the bottle was small and out of place, more like those ampules that carried drops of a saint's blood.

Annoyed with Fina and her late preoccupation with forged beauty, she went straight to the kitchen and asked Martinella for some sweet cakes. As she sat nibbling near the kitchen hearth, a heavy knock came to the kitchen's canalside door where the *palazzo* accepted its deliveries. Tonia promptly answered it and greeted two men carrying reedy baskets filled with hay. The first to enter looked to be in his late fifties. The dark hair above his ears was starting to turn silver and his face was filled with black and grey stubble. He smiled when he saw Martinella in the room and went to kiss the old woman on her soft cheeks before sharing the contents of his basket with her. The second to enter was a far younger man, and judging by his looks, was the son of the first. Mafalda was struck by his attractive face and pleasing physique. She stood up from her stool, dry flakes of pastry falling from her lips. She licked her mouth, apricot, and spontaneously wondered what *his* mouth tasted like before swallowing her last bite.

Martinella appeared quite satisfied with her order of plump oysters. Filed between the layers of cushiony dried field grass were nestled over fifty of the shellfish, and presumably the second of the two baskets contained the same. The House of Orso consumed as much fruit of the sea as any other noble house in Venice; it was delivered to their door daily during the late mornings, everything freshly harvested from the waters. Tonia took away the first basket to scrub the contents in preparation for the evening meal as Martinella introduced her longtime vendors to Mafalda. Santino the father and Baldovino the son. It was just as she thought.

Santino was loud and hearty, someone who was certain to always be in high spirits and drawing out those emotions in others. Baldovino was quieter, more guarded with only a soft smile on his face. She could feel his dark eyes move over her as she observed Santino knife open an oyster and serve it to Martinella, who gulped down the living delicacy. The father quickly scolded his son for not offering to do the same for the beautiful young woman of the house. Baldovino appeared in his mid-twenties, older than she and already mature in the world as men his age were. He didn't laugh or become shy by his father's coaxing, nor did he jump to the task. He was a very different sort of creature from his father.

Santino quickly offered Martinella a show of what else he had in his boat for the day, as she might find something more that she'd care to serve to the family, or perhaps even a few fat and succulent fish to roast with herbs for the servants. Left alone, Baldovino eventually moved closer and pushed some hay around in his basket as if in search for just the right oyster; his hand came up empty. Looking to Mafalda, who patiently stood shifting from one foot to the other, he smiled with some secret thought and then excused himself. She watched as he walked out of the door to where the others had gone, soon to return. Coming to stand before her once more, he held out a large mollusk, far more generous in size than the ones they regularly ate. It was a fine catch, a basket of those would fetch an excellent price, especially on a feast day when the noble houses were entertaining guests and wanted to impress. Pulling a sharp knife from his belt, he sliced between the shells and carefully pried the animal open, discarding the top of the oyster's case to a table. Skilled, he swiftly cut beneath the meat and detached its membrane to make it easier to consume. He smiled once more and carefully handed over the plump, briny offering.

Mafalda was embarrassed, the oyster was rather big and she felt hesitant to swallow it before Baldovino. Oysters were said to cause passions in the eaters; she was certain he knew that. As well he stood close enough that she swore she could feel the heat radiating from his body, though it could have just been the kitchen blaze. He watched her expectantly, almost eagerly, standing tall enough to look over her. She wanted to move away, but only far enough so that she could spy on this man unnoticed; he was very desirable. He wiped his knife upon a rag hanging at his hip and slipped it back into his belt.

Tentatively accepting the halved shell, the size of which completely engulfed her palm, she looked meekly up at Baldovino and then slowly brought the vessel closer to her lips. Just as she was about to tilt the creature's hull up to slide the oyster into her mouth, he whispered for her to wait. She paused short and her eyes grew large. She began to blush. Why had he stopped her? She didn't want to prolong this. Martinella would be back soon, or Tonia might catch an eyeful of the two and Mafalda felt that the man was standing too close, too familiarly. Carefully taking back the shell from her, he again pulled out his knife and scrapped delicately at the flesh, quickly exposing a large and glistening white orb. It was a pearl, a very large pearl. Baldovino had gone out to the boat for this prized catch on purpose, he must have guessed that it looked right to contain one of these beloved seeds. Mafalda gasped and her lips curled up in a delighted smile, her face filled with surprise. As the voices of the others came to ear from close at the kitchen door, and as Tonia turned from her workbench to burn some spoiled hay in the fire, Baldovino quickly thrust the oyster's flesh into his mouth and swirled the meat around while casting away the shell. In the blink of an eye, he produced the pearl between his lips, took it from his mouth and handed it to Mafalda.

This was erotic. She felt short of breath and excited as Santino called for his son from the door. And in an instant, Baldovino was gone. She stood clenching the precious object in her hand until Martinella kindly told her to get to; she needed to get back to cooking and didn't need a fine dress in her way. Noble ladies weren't meant to hang around the kitchen, and they weren't meant for fishermen's sons either, the old woman whispered with a wrinkly wink. Mafalda plucked up another apricot delight, squeezed the matron's hand, and went out to ponder such a meeting in a loftier part of the *palazzo*.

Mirella

She'd lived well enough during the span of nearly twenty-five years with her husband. He didn't mount every young wench in Venice; neither had he employed one of its celebrated courtesans. If Mirella were to bet all his great wealth, she'd place it on the assumption that he'd never bedded another woman *in* the city since her arrival in *Venezia* all those years ago. This had saved her from those common humiliations that her fellow noblewomen encountered. There was nothing worse than entertaining the courtesan your husband was compensating at one's own entertainments, those banquets that were hosted by every esteemed wife of very rich and powerful lords. Orso *had* had a hot temper, but he'd never abused her, with physical acts or with vile words.

He'd been a passionate lover, had frequently whispered quiet admirations into her ears whenever they crossed paths in the house. He covered her with adornments and sent her gifts, he flattered her, he played with her, and he watched her with an eager eye. He'd fallen in love with her. Perhaps not the day they'd wed; whether it was Lagia or Mirella to be his wife may not have initially made much difference to him. They were both handsome, agreeable women. No, he'd fallen for her after the nuptials, as she became familiar with his *palazzo*, and his bed, in Venice. Orso's father had been so rich as to acquire a second home, a wedding gift to his only son. A prominent reputation for the clever and energetic heir quickly flourished. They'd always been a powerful family, but the House of Orso soon grew even more prosperous than the house of its predecessor.

She'd fallen in love with him as well, and he became both a beloved husband and *inamorato*. She had put away those passing, callow passions for Remo, her only other lover. With those encounters retired, she embraced Venetian life. Venice was a gilded isle, and her husband one of its most influential citizens. However, when Fina was eventually born and placed into her arms, Mirella failed to develop any strong affection while gazing into the face of her patrician daughter. Could anyone have seen into her heart and exposed her dismal attitudes toward motherhood, they would have also glimpsed there, developing resentments for Orso, though on the outside she went on displaying ardency. And with the subsequent births of three more daughters whom she loved no more than the first, Mirella's affinity for her husband dwindled further, though she remained artful in keeping her feelings disguised.

Soon after her wedding, Severiano died with sudden pains in his chest. Mirella believed that arctic hearts like her father's were destined to seize up in a terrible way and wasn't sorry to hear of it. Liborio inherited the land, and from this brother's wife Gostanza, Mirella sporadically heard word of her childhood grounds and the keepers of it. Remo's father eventually retired to his wife and a quiet cottage, charging Remo to tend to Liborio's land. Remo went on to be just as consistent, tending to the family's holdings with care, until he came to leave unexpectedly. No one ever heard from him again and he eventually faded into the past. Mirella assumed he'd become a steward elsewhere, had taken a wife, had had children in number. Perhaps even, he no longer lived.

But then one day, all these years later, a servant showed a merchant into the *palazzo* and into Orso's chamber to speak of business. Mirella being in her husband's den, quickly passed out of the room to leave the men to their discussions when *that* face, more aged yet eternally tempting, flashed before her eyes. His dress was sumptuous, threaded with gold, dotted with gems; a yellow pearl hung from one of his ears.

Questions pealed through her ears like church bells. What was Remo doing here and how could he afford such finery? Was this a ploy to see her? Certainly that was improbable. Was this the beginnings of some twisted revenge for her having so quickly married another, decades ago? Completely implausible; and he hadn't even known about her pregnancy, or the failing of it. She wasn't even convinced that he'd loved her back then. She was simply a young fruit in the vineyard for the picking, however dangerous it was for the son of a hired man to pluck it. And she had been *willing*, with or without true affection.

She stood without Orso's door as the men conversed, their words only an animated babble. Nervousness, fear, anticipation, and heat sped through her veins. She could feel blood pulsing in her neck and bosom. A salacious memory came rushing to mind of one feverous pushing between her thighs on a humid summer night in the vineyard, so many years before. *Why* had Remo visited the House of Orso?

Paola

Paola had experienced pain before this, for she'd always been susceptible to bad foods, cold drafts that brought on a month of congestion, and even uncommon but irritating headaches that swept in over the slightest stresses and kept her bedridden for a day. This perhaps was why she loved Martinella so much; the old woman was like a doting grandmother. Mirella wasn't inclined to nurse a daughter through any physical hardships. But Martinella was always kind, bringing her strengthening broths and toasted bread, rubbing her frozen toes when she was weak with fever, or singing to her when she was wheezy, and labored with her breath. Paola didn't believe herself to be inherently weak, just more susceptible to ailments than her sisters. What could she do? Whatever passed them by clung to her. But in spite of being through much before, her pains this time were far more severe.

Nothing was explained when she'd first woken. Therefore, who knew how long she'd been unconscious; a day, two? And how had she become so ill by poison? How had she ingested it? Not a word was spoken while she remained quarantined to her rest. At the very least, she had Martinella's sweet wrinkly face, sensibility, and wholesome cooking to carry her through. In recalling her poisonous raptures, she weakly asked her elderly companion the name of the man who worked for her father. Who was the gentle sir who had carried her? His name was Thorello; indisputably paid a healthy sum by Orso as one of his men, though Martinella knew little else. But one thing Paola knew; her father trusted him, as he did very few other men with his business dealings.

She slept a great deal after her first awakening, and dreamt several times of Thorello cradling her as they traveled down long, warmly lit corridors. He whispered into the lustrous locks of her black hair, kissing her, and wishing her a sweet sleep. Once inevitably placed in her bed, she'd slumber while he placed fruit and marzipan and dulcet notes by her bedside. Those dreams were a comfort and a respite from those other nightmares. From fleeing down a darkened path to the sounds of muffled cries, with a large shadowy figure at her heels. When she regained her strength, perhaps she might see Thorello again.

After several more days had passed, any lingering pain in her stomach subsided and she began to feel better, despite continual fatigue and a sweat that dampened her nightgowns. The stinking poison was taking leave through her skin. She consumed only fortifying red wine and soups, straight from Martinella's hand. But it was as she was handed one such wooden bowl on the cusp of her recovery, that she noticed a strange odor not of her own body. Something repugnant that hinted of sickness. Looking at the old woman's outstretched hand, there was a length of linen wrapped around it; she'd seen it in the last days but had thought little about it. Martinella was probably covering a burn or a cut. But this time, she noted a yellow-brown splotch seeping through the top of the bandage and a faint red streak under the woman's skin that ran up from the dressing, over her wrist and onwards.

"*Martinella*, your hand! What has happened to it?" Paola blurted, deeply concerned.

"Ah, tis' nothing but the errant nip of a knife. I'll go have a wash of it now. Tis' nothing. Rest you, child." She replied.

With that, she exited the room. Paola knew it was worse than a slight cut and that the disguised wound wasn't healing; it was infected. Whoever next entered her chamber, she'd solicit them to look in on Martinella and see what could be done for her hand. But no one did come into her room for many hours.

She felt lonely, but resting comfortably, she fell asleep once more.

When she opened her eyes again, night had fallen and there was a hearty fire heating her room from the fireplace. Martinella sat in a chair not far off, her head sunken down upon her chest like a goose nestled in its fluffed feathers, asleep. Paola would get up slowly and sneak over to her to spy upon her hand and see if a fresh bandage had been applied. Perhaps she could even lift the cotton to view just how festered the wound might be.

Even as warm as the chamber was, as she pushed her blankets away, she felt a chill flood over her damp sleeping gown and she shivered. The cold of the stones permeated up from under the ornate rug as she placed her bare feet on the ground. Standing up took a moment of effort; she was still weak but sensed she'd be completely recovered in just a few days more. Toeing over to the old woman as quietly as was possible, she stopped to observe such a peaceful repose. Martinella always worked so hard; it seemed time that she should retire to the home of one of her children, or even grandchildren. Her husband had passed on long ago; Paola had never met him. She didn't know what she'd do without the woman's tender touch and their intimate prattle once she left the House of Orso. She knew she needed Martinella. If Paola had been a betrothed woman, she'd have asked Martinella to come with her to her new home, particularly if she hadn't another happier, more comfortable place elsewhere.

Leaning down to the woman, whose hands were crossed and motionless over the apron covering her lap, Paola reached out to push back her long sleeve as gently as possible to get a better view of the partially exposed bandage; it was newly changed and unspoiled. Yet, on brushing Martinella's hand, it was morbidly pale except for the now, even thicker, fiery red streak running up from the cotton cover. The skin was cold and not as soft as she expected. Paola was too surprised to look beneath the bandage and backed away.

"Martinella." she whispered. "Madame? *Nonnina*?" Her words grew increasingly distressed as she repeated them, becoming louder and louder.

The woman did not stir. Fear moved in Paola's gut. She hoped that this was just a deep slumber, come on from how fatigued Martinella must be after waiting on her young ward these past days. She stepped forward again and said her name forcefully. Paola was angry now for having to feel so frightened when she wasn't feeling well; she didn't need another scare. Delicately nudging the woman's shoulder, the body felt unnatural and stiff. Paola didn't want to accept something that was so obviously certain. Her skin began to tingle uncomfortably as though pricked repeatedly by pins and her ears felt stuffed with cloth; she could hear nothing except for a steady ringing. Standing tall and turning away, she faced the door and walked towards it, expressionless, shocked. She needed to get help.

Fina

Dressed in black, as was her mother's demand, with several sprigs of fragrant rosemary pinned on her sleeve for mourning, Fina went to speak to Noemi. Though circumstances were very worrying, she felt that it was premature the way their mother had demanded that they accept their father's death. What did Noemi think of this? Perhaps it wasn't the plague; maybe he had met with some accident and was recovering somewhere, with some village family. He might have fallen off his horse. Most villagers couldn't write their own names, this *must* be the reason they'd had no word. It was late in the evening, and by going directly to Noemi's chamber while the house was quiet, perhaps she could also find out whether or not her sister was receiving letters from Rodolfo and if their mother had been pressuring her in any way for an alliance.

Lit by only a few dim sconces that threw shadows up onto the cool marble walls, Fina was surprised to see Paola out of bed in only a thin cotton shift and standing statuelike down the hall at a distance. As the candlelight flickered in their snug holders, it cast the girl in an eerie light. She was standing with her back to

Fina, her black hair falling loosely as she swayed ever so slightly from side to side with her head hanging down and her arms crossed around her body. Fina wondered if she was walking in her sleep; very possible with only the fretful rest the poor sparrow had been experiencing with her recent illness. This was yet another matter of great concern. How had Paola become ill with poison in the first place? It was clear that she'd only consumed little of the toxin, for otherwise she'd have proven far sicker.

Fina had been upset to learn that Noemi had found a fruit from the deadly nightshade plant in the hallway before their father's door. She was even more irritated to hear Martinella inform their mother of it. Even some of Orso's men had been present. After all, it had been Fina herself who had dropped that damned berry. She'd only secured three of those black orbs from Aurelia. Courtesans carefully diluted the juices and dotted them in their eyes to expand the pupils and make them look large and shiny, a quality that men found attractive. She needed to start practicing, and had secretly visited her friend to obtain a few, a visit that was now against her mother's wishes. Those berries were hard to come by, as most apothecaries assumed you were making such a purchase to poison your husband or your husband's lover. When Fina became a courtesan, she'd seek out a gold-greedy gardener for future provisions.

On returning to her chamber from that private outing, one of the three fruits was not to be found in the carefully folded handkerchief that she'd so delicately carried them in. It caused her some anxiety; the berries were *very* poisonous. If she'd dropped one on the walk home, a child in their innocence could have picked it up. Most certainly a roving dog would. Should either have put it in their mouth, it would bring them quite near to death. For the littlest ones, just two berries accidently consumed off of that flowering plant was all that was necessary to send them into God's arms. She hadn't even thought that she may have dropped it *in* the house and was glad that Martinella had pitched it into the canal. Of course, Fina was not willing to divulge that the berry had been hers; it would have given away her plans to join Aurelia as a courtesan.

She disliked such secrecy, but had no intention of being sent to a nunnery. Fina had felt suspicious that this was what their mother would soon be planning for her daughters, though Noemi might be spared. She couldn't despise Mirella for considering such a plan however, for this was the way in Venice. Noble families daily sent a flock of daughters into the nunneries. Only, understanding that this was an eventuality and that she was unlikely to be *the* chosen daughter for marriage, Fina couldn't help but make plans to intervene on her own behalf.

In any case, the lost berry didn't matter any longer. It wasn't what had caused Paola's illness and it had been dispatched. It couldn't do anyone any harm now. So what had provoked her little sister to become so ill? Was it possible that Paola had been sipping from a poisonous draft, hurting herself? With their father's frighteningly long absence and their mother's painful aloofness, had Paola secured some exotic tincture from the market stalls? Certainly none of her sisters could ever be found to be so capricious? But then again, Fina had been keeping secrets. Why not any of them?

As she approached, she discovered the reason for Paola's standing so oddly in the dimness of the night. There was someone lying on the floor before her. Hurrying around Paola, she saw that it was Tonia. The servant lay motionless with her eyes open wide, her pupils so dilated that they were almost entirely black. Her face was as pale as the hem of Paola's nightdress and her mouth was set in a pained, open twist. Her lips were covered in pinkish-red foam. The sight was horribly unsettling, the girl no longer with the living. Had she slipped and hit her head on the stones? Kneeling down to check, Fina ordered Paola to go for Martinella. Her little sister, looking as ghostly and grieved as ever, shook her head 'no'.

"She won't come, she's *gone*." Paola whispered, her voice quavering.

"Gone? What do you mean?" Fina asked with a demanding tone.

A vision of fleeing servants came into her mind, suddenly reminded of the looming threat of plague. Quickly searching Tonia over, she saw that the stout servant girl was squeezing something in her fist. Carefully opening her hand, she found four hard and little objects, yellow and sticky in Tonia's palm.

"Oh, *oh* Fina!" Paola looked away and around into the shadows, unnerved and terrified. Soon peering back down to Fina, the youngest nearly hissed the words. "*In...her...hand*. Those are the lemon sweets mother gave *me*."

A sickening feeling crept into Fina's stomach as she regarded her sister, who had clearly entered a state of shock. "Paola...did *you*, recently, eat of this confection?"

Mirella

The House of Orso had met with tragedy, but Mirella had every intention of remaining impervious to its effects. She wasn't going to alter the timeline of her plans for lost servants, or panic over pockets of plague that might soon die out, or even allow herself to remember that she actually once loved the husband that was now gone forever. Pushing every anxiety out of her mind, she focused on what needed to be done. As Orso wasn't coming back, she now had absolute rule over their children, their home and their wealth. She would need to manage this properly.

Poor Martinella, a festering wound, an injury received in the kitchen no doubt. Certainly she'd had a great many such cuts before, with all her years cooking for noble families. Unfortunately, the woman had been very old and this clumsy slice had been her last. Though Mirella felt sorry for her, it seemed that in spite of the infection that had made its way into her blood, she'd at least had the luxury of dozing off into her eternal sleep. That was far better than the sufferings that were beginning to occur from without the *palazzo* walls. The house had received word from vendors making their morning deliveries. Whisperings of which neighborhoods had seen a death. The plague was indeed visiting Venice, but Mirella couldn't be sure that it would take hold.

As for Tonia, Mirella could only conclude that the girl had swallowed poison to kill herself. She announced this as fact to the rest of the servants and to her daughters. She also believed that it was Tonia to have dropped the nightshade berry; the wicked girl had visited a seller of such plants at the market. Even when closely questioning Paola if the servant had ever left her alone at the market stalls, it could not be denied. In fact, Tonia had irritably moved off to seek an ointment when last they'd been, though Paola hadn't thought to ask her what the medicine was for.

Mirella settled that Tonia had been very unhappy, even ill, also worrying herself to death after receiving news of the plague. Further, after having the servant girl's room searched, items belonging to Paola were found. Tonia had not only been morose, but jealous too. It was decided that Tonia had been the source of Paola's suffering.

Noemi and Mafalda appeared persuaded that Tonia had taken her own life, and had sickened their sister. Paola and Fina on the other hand, acted nervously, as though some undiscovered culprit lurked behind the tapestried walls. When pried however, they could not offer any reason why suicide wasn't the cause for Tonia's death. Mirella had questioned hard; had there been *anything* else they'd heard or seen to make them believe otherwise? They both swore that there hadn't been.

Mirella ended the investigation and melted sealing wax over it. Both of the servants were promptly buried in the courtyard garden, though a priest was not requested to give blessings over their makeshift graves. The business of being called to the homes of the ailing would now expose holy men to the pestilence; they could not risk one's entry into their house.

Mirella now waited patiently for Remo. She'd made discreet inquiries, discovering that he'd become very rich in trade. The man now oversaw his *own* estate, in Padova. He was a widower, the union having ended without any living children. He currently maintained a favorable dwelling on the island, a recent purchase. She had no trouble believing his good fortune; he'd been intelligent and hardworking all those many years ago.

Mirella still didn't know what his conversation had been with her husband, just before Orso's final departure, but she had no difficulty guessing the secret reason for his visit. Now wealthy and unrestrained, he sought pleasure in Venice! Hadn't he come to tempt her into being his mistress? What a thrill, what a triumph, to entangle himself with such an eminent beauty, such a reputable noblewoman! Whatever words were exchanged, his visit to Orso had been a pretense. He'd proposed a business relationship, but only in order to gain entry into the house. Orso had known Remo from her father's vineyard, as well Remo remained employed with her brother Liborio following their father's death. Orso would look on him as trustworthy, completely unaware of any past intimate connections. Of that, only Lagia had been unwittingly privy.

Mirella was now making it a point to look her absolute best, for sooner than later, Remo would return. It lately infuriated her when her lady's attendant, however overworked, piled her hair in a haphazard arrangement. She taught her a lesson by making her do it over again, on more than one occasion, a waste of time with so many other pressing duties. That servant was no longer paid from the coffers. When recently dropping a glass goblet, the noise shattered Mirella's nerves and the woman was immediately sent away. During uneasy times, such irritations could not be borne.

But now, with Orso's disappearance, she might be *more* than a mistress to Remo. It was due time that Fina, Mafalda and Paola take their places with the nuns. There, they would be out of the way and of little expense to her. She had of course observed that Fina was getting bold these days. An infatuation with the storied lives of Venice's courtesans? Mirella knew that she was a clever girl; Fina had guessed her future and was making plans to escape it. Keeping Fina away from Aurelia, fallen and ignoble, had been only a temporary solution. She certainly couldn't chance a daughter's circumventing the nunnery, only to publicly prostitute herself. Such a profession could also compromise Mirella's fortune should Fina ever find herself full with a noble bastard's son. No, she would have three daughters enclosed, and as quickly as possible too.

As for Noemi, that girl had grown strangely determined as well. Fina thought she'd seen Mirella ride out at night in a gondola, but it was not so. Mirella had also spied the cloaked one from her own chamber window, glimpsing an amber flash of hair in the moonlight from beneath that hood. It had been Noemi. Had it been other times, Mirella would have interrogated, even threatened the girl, until she confessed to where she'd been. She couldn't bide a bastard child from *any* of her daughters. But because of the timing, it was of little consequence; she'd have Noemi married to Rodolfo within weeks. If she were pregnant even now, on account of a secret lover, she could easily pass the child off as his. Such a marriage would have met with opposition from Orso. But now that he was gone, it would prove an excellent arrangement, keeping Mirella's estate profitably aligned with one of the richest noble families in *Venezia*. With everyone tucked away and a mass of wealth to keep her comfortable for all of her days, why not also take on a fine and prosperous new husband, guaranteed to give her pleasure?

It had grown frustrating that she'd had no word from him at all since that single visit. And even during that surprising encounter, there hadn't been any words between them. To wait caused her to become easily agitated with the servants, her daughters, and especially any vendors that lately hassled her about commissions. Why had her husband placed so many costly orders before his last passage? Why an additional gondola? Had they not enough? A great many expensive requests were keeping the tradesmen calling. She began to terminate these agreements, even arguing with established men of business in the doorway. Mirella wasn't the least bit parsimonious, but there was just no use for Orso's final and inexplicable whims. She began sending goods back without even glancing at what had been delivered. Her excuse was that she was in mourning for her husband. The vendors could sell their commissions to other nobles with less current grievances.

Restless to see him in the *palazzo* once more, she considered sending Remo an invitation to dine. If so extended, it would be prudent to invite others too, to avoid the stirring of rumors so soon after her husband's death. The plague however, made a gathering insupportable. She began to doubt that his visit with Orso had had any secret meaning at all. What places her imagination had taken her! But then a letter came. Her name, written in his bold hand upon the smooth paper, sent her heart racing. It arrived two days after the burial of Martinella and Tonia. Paola was recovered, and all of Mirella's intended arrangements for her children were under way. As for Remo, he'd requested a meeting. He *did* wish to see her. How her bosom rose and fell with excitement, her mind and body welcoming his attentions more fervently than before.

Noemi

She read Ilario's letter in the privacy of her chamber and was astonished to discover that he had noticed her frequent passing, and sometimes lingering, across from his shop. Though the woman he saw was veiled, he could still catch glimpses of the beautiful color of her hair radiating through the lace. He began to recognize her by her slow pace and her figure, when he happened to be outside or when he glanced out of an open window at just the right time.

One day, after she'd passed by, he followed her and her lady servant at a distance. They'd slipped into one of Venice's great churches and he'd trailed along behind them. The attendant had not knelt down to prayer, but was wandering around the circumference of the house, intently viewing the rich artwork. He had no trouble getting the information he sought. Holding his cap in his hands, he'd humbly approached the servant and asked if she wasn't the daughter of the neighborhood baker. Wouldn't she deliver best regards to her father from the gondola maker? Engaged with a rather gruesome rendition of the plague, she'd startled and then quickly corrected him. She was employed in the House of Orso, and of no relation to the baker!

Ilario made his apologies and walked away. That was all the information he'd needed.

Soon after, he discovered her name. She was the only redheaded one of Orso's daughters, so it wasn't very difficult. He would have eventually found a way to meet her, but ironic good fortune expedited that moment when he received a commission from the man of the house himself, bringing him to stand before her. After that first greeting, when he'd followed behind a reticent Noemi as she led him to her father, he wanted to reach out and touch her. He wanted to bury his face in her hair, to slide his hands around her waist and pull her closer. She was so beautiful, blessed with a smile so tender that he'd ached to kiss her lips.

He'd never transacted with Orso before, but had heard that he was fair, albeit a challenge. If Ilario could gain this man's trust, and show him that he was worthy, perhaps there was a chance that he'd be allowed to court Noemi. However, at present there had been rumors. Orso had been gone for some months on one of his regular trade routes. Without return and without any word, his wife had lately donned darker shades. Claims that he'd been struck with the pestilence had been circulating. The world of Venice was small and news of nobles spread quickly. Ilario wouldn't have thought much of this gossip, for death was as common as birth all the world over. Only now, the name of this particular family meant much more to him. He prayed that it was not true.

With the plague so near, the climate in Venice was changing. Many citizens were scared. He wanted Noemi to know that he loved her, in spite of their hardly knowing one another. He knew the moment he'd followed her into her house, that he would follow her anywhere. Of course, he was uncertain of her feelings. But watching her pass his home so many times, so gentle a creature turned in his direction, he had a small hope. Had she any thought for him, or was it merely a curiosity for the making of gondolas? Should he risk sending her more letters? Would she permit him to see her once more, privately?

With unsteady hands and her heart full, she crafted a reply that was careful, yet left no doubt that their feelings were aligned. To get it into his hands, she knew that she'd have to be very bold. Instead of walking on her usual side of the canal across from his workshop, she strolled directly before his house and dropped the letter into a fresh nest of woodchips. He'd seen her from his window, his shutters open wide. She'd secretly hoped he'd be watching and waiting for her, and he was. Moments later, he snatched up her answer. She was already gone down the *calle*, her maidservant trailing behind her, looking bored but none the wiser of what her mistress had deposited at his door.

Feigning to practice her painting each day, she was hardly able to concentrate with such feelings of anticipation pulsing through her body. Soon, a second letter was delivered. Boating past, he smiled for his beloved and never a happier expression was returned. Looking first to see that no other boatmen were near, he dropped a sealed note upon the stone steps as he drifted past. When it was safe, she toed quickly over and down to retrieve it. This message was even more amorous, but also held news of misfortune.

Having read the plans meant for Orso, Mirella had decided to cancel the order for the gondola, a precious commission that would have bolstered Ilario's income and reputation. She'd written an eloquent paragraph concerning her certainty about her husband's death. Now in mourning, she would not feel right to continue such commercial endeavors as if Orso was well and with them all.

Ilario's letter to Noemi went on to propose that they meet. Only, if he were found at the *palazzo* without a valid reason, it could be disastrous for them both. But, if she could find a way to come to him secretly, perhaps they could spend a little time in one another's company without anyone knowing. During the day, her visit would be seen; neighbors watched all the comings and goings along the canals. But in the night, perhaps she could make her way to him; he wasn't very far. He assured her of his true intentions. How he waited night and day to hear her voice again. If they were to meet however, they needed to make haste, for the sickness was drawing nearer.

Ilario was not the only one to remind her of the encroaching plague. People were speaking of it more and more. No deaths had been reported in Venice, and yet visibly less boats were careening through the canals, while fewer vendors hawked at the markets. If the pestilence *was* making its way, it meant Noemi and Ilario had only a little time. Once the Black Death entered Venice, it wouldn't be long before Mirella locked the family in to wait it out. Not even a letter would pass through the doors. She knew they *must* see each other, and soon. This was how Noemi found herself disguised by mask and hood, entering an unfamiliar gondola late one night. The driver, a trusted friend of Ilario's, promised to deliver her safely.

Mafalda

Weak and unsteady, Mafalda teetered over to the boat. She would have to pull it up even further on land than it was to avoid stepping into the icy waters to board the craft, for she wasn't steady enough to climb in at the tip that rested on the sand. Even if she had been, she'd have landed on the corpse and would lose her footing. Bending over, she thought the strain of pulling the rowboat further ashore would be her end. The blood drying on her guilty hand, sticky and slippery, did not aid her cold, swollen fingers in the task of gripping. She was in terrible pain.

Mafalda couldn't look at the woman in the belly of the boat, too afraid that she would forget the last of her courage. She was certain it was Noemi, one of her treasured sisters. After a few pathetically futile hauls, the vessel was as squarely on land as Mafalda would be able to get it, especially considering the weight it toted. Exhausted, she sank to the ground and sat, motionlessly looking out over the waves toward the city of Venice in the distance. But soon her eyes darted back to the bobbing boat. Snowflakes began to fall more steadily, blanketing the lifeless and delicate head of gold. Mafalda had survived the plague and had killed a man, but could she survive *this*?

Standing, she hobbled around to the side of the craft and carefully placed one leg over. She'd forgotten that her feet were bare until one was planted firmly onto the floor next to the body. A horrible pain shot up through her leg. She hadn't stepped on anything to cause it; it was nothing more than her being awkwardly mobile in such a perilous condition. If she survived, she knew there was a chance she'd lose her toes. However excruciating, she leaned all her weight on the foot and carefully swung the other one inside. Crouching down, she delayed by admiring the glossy cream fabric that clothed the body, the perfectly stitched folds of the gown beginning to collect pockets of snow. She reached out her unsullied hand and gently pushed the stiff head sideways until it exposed the pale face and blank stare. It was a woman she did not recognize.

She wanted to vomit; she wanted to cry. A rush of numbing adrenaline rose once more in her body. Concentrating, she pilfered the slippers from off of the dead woman's feet and with every last effort she had, first the legs, next the torso and then the pretty red tresses, pushed the body out of the boat. Its upper half sunk into the water while its bare feet rested on the sand.

It was gruesome and unconscionable. The noblewoman deserved a caring burial, as did *everyone* on this island of death. But Mafalda could not be the one to give it to them. She quickly made the sign of the cross over her body and then glanced around. Discovering two oars in the bottom of the boat, she sat down at the front end and used one to push against the shallow sand beneath the waves and paddle off. She hadn't the strength to row with both of the oars. One alone was already far too heavy.

It wasn't with physical strength that she began to make her way toward Venice, but rather and only by a mere flicker of spirit. How easy it would be to go adrift in this vessel, floating out to sea, falling asleep beneath a blanket of snow. How was she to know what she would find if she made it back? She might discover such horrors that it would have been better to slip away just now, when her eyes were so heavy. But as the boat rocked, she remembered the words her sister had said to her in her dream. Fina had told her to open her eyes, and with that warning, Mafalda had bore up in her grave. It was an omen that she must live, must *try* to live. And so, she paddled onward, toward whatever awaited her.

A Mother's Rule

Her expectancy grew hour by hour over the reunion that would take place that very evening. Mirella felt all the more elated knowing that she had abstained from being the first to break the silence. She hadn't given in to the delay by sending a dinner invitation to Remo. He'd sent a letter first, the one she knew must come. She was greatly pleased, feeling that she'd gained some unnamed advantage.

Her hands shook imperceptibly when she'd read his letter. The message was brief, but of course he would be careful until he knew her feelings. It contained the simple request of an audience with her. Today, he would have it. But first, with Paola now fully able to sit up with her sisters, it was time for Mirella to apprise her daughters of her plans for their futures.

It went surprisingly easy. To symbolize her rule, she'd called them in to sit before her in Orso's meeting chamber. Mirella hadn't stepped into the room since her husband had left the morning of his final departure. It was now dusty with neglect. That sunny dawn, she'd entered the room alone to wish him a safe journey, shutting the door behind her. He'd quickly bent her over the spacious wooden table scattered with papers, lifted her skirts and delivered a lusty thumping. When she thought of it, she smiled. Did she miss him? His papers drifting to the floor, her husband's breathless exertions, his strong grasping. She cleared her throat; that was the past, and a man she'd fallen out of love with long ago. Today, she was looking ahead to a different future.

She'd had to instruct one of the male servants to use force on the locked door for her entry, next ordering him to light a fire in the dim cavern. When all four of the girls were finally sitting before her, she couldn't help but feel sorry for them. Or at the very least, three of them; Noemi didn't deserve any pity. She'd soon be married and amply rich. After hearing the news, they all sat speechless. Fina's face radiated defiance, her mouth forming a bitter smirk. Once enclosed, Mirella was certain such a wild attitude would be tamed. She was secretly sorry for it however, Fina was so much like she was in her youth.

Mafalda had stared blankly at her lap as she fiddled with a milky pearl hanging from her neck. Mirella couldn't recognize it, but due to its size thought it was a mock bauble picked up from one of the many trinket vendors to be found in Venice. She wouldn't be able to keep such ornaments where she was going.

Further, Mirella would be selling Fina's, Mafalda's and Paola's more expensive belongings, of which they owned many. Their father had spoiled them, and it would now support their meager lives in the convent. Substantial less would be drained from the coffers for their needs.

Noemi stared off toward a window. Her eyes were glossy and her expression simple and sad. *Ah! But wasn't that what happened when you fell in love with a knave who wasn't noble and would never be given a chance to ask for your hand?* This was only an assumption. Mirella did not know the man's identity, or even if Noemi indeed concealed a secret lover. It didn't matter.

Paola went oddly still, her face as pale as though she were still suffering from the effects of the poison. Her skin juxtaposed dramatically against her dark head. She stared directly at her mother with such a deadpan expression as to be considered creepy. The creature was becoming quite thin, having lost more weight than she could afford over those days of her illness. Even with her youthful prettiness, and even with that allure in her dark eyes, she was just too waifish to be presented for a marriage contract. Any suitor would take one look at her and know that she wouldn't survive her first birthing bed. But gaunt and frail would be suitable for a nun; they'd employ her to weep and pray for the souls of Venice. Perhaps they might even put her to work in the kitchen or the garden; the labor would build up her narrow frame.

As she looked the girls over in their silent state, a motherly tenderness snuck over her once more. Couldn't she be compelled to change her mind, their eyes said? In that moment, she might have reached out to squeeze their hands, could have assured them that everything would be well, would have made promises that they could stay at home and marry the men they would someday come to love. But the sentiment lasted only a second. She reminded herself for the hundredth time that this was how things were done. Sucking in the swift and confident breath of the unaffected, Mirella ordered the girls to their chambers where they could take their evening meals in solitude. It would do them good to reflect upon and accept, their futures. Excluding Noemi, they should write letters to their friends, send word of their good fortunes. They were being gifted the opportunity to live pious, godly lives. Noemi must wait to share her deep appreciation for the match her mother had made for her, until the marriage contract was signed. With that, the sisters stood and silently filed out of their father's chamber, each moving their separate ways as they stepped over the threshold.

Mirella now had a meeting with her first lover to prepare for, an occasion to take place just after nightfall. She would serve him a rich dinner. She would wear her most beautiful gown and let her hair fall loosely, adorned with gold netting and pearls. She was filled with youth and vigor just thinking about it. How she would excite Remo with her charms! She would seduce him as easily as she had those many years ago; just the very thing he was undeniably seeking.

During her husband's absence, Mirella had kept Orso's business connections pacified and all of their noble allies close. If she were to marry Remo, he could nurture her holdings into an even greater empire. Before long, she would be *the* wealthiest woman in Venice. She was beginning to feel like the most desired and powerful too.

Noemi

She hadn't missed her mother's subtle pressures for her to be kind to Rodolfo, but then again, Mirella had encouraged them all to be cheerful and bright before their guests. In spite of her father's worryingly long departure, her mother had continued to have some small entertainments and dinners in the *palazzo*. Noemi had supposed that Mirella was working to assure the noble families of Venice that the House of Orso was still in order and that their patriarch was only delayed. But a terrible reality remained; Orso continued to go unaccounted for and Mirella was acting hyper and artificial.

Why had no lines of worry creased their mother's face? Mirella had certainly loved her husband. Wasn't that clear? They were magnetic to watch together! Noemi had witnessed it all her life, could *see* that they had loved one another. Of course, one could never know what transpired behind chamber doors, but even so, she just couldn't imagine that there had been any division between them. Perhaps trying to remain strong was having an unusual effect on Mirella's behavior. Did she keep busy and smiling to keep hope in her heart? It pained Noemi to consider these uneasy questions. How she prayed for Orso's hasty return, most especially for their poor mother's sake.

Noemi needed to see Ilario again. Their greatest fear had come true; the plague had finally washed ashore. So far, Noemi didn't know any of the houses and the deaths had been few. But to look out over the quiet *calli* was an eerie thing. The plague was an unpredictable foe. It could destroy a city in a flash, or it could sputter out in a fortnight. She was afraid, but rather than it making her cautious to go out, her spirit grew increasingly foolhardy and resolute. With so much uncertainty at home and throughout the city, the only solid thing in the world for her was Ilario.

Noemi affectionately recalled the first and only other night they'd had together. Dropped from the gondola a short distance down the canal from his home, she'd swiftly slipped down the thin *calle*, going like a shadow until she reached the back door of his workshop. Lightly knocking on the cedar, *fate, fate, fate* was all she heard beneath her knuckles. Ilario lived alone, and he was expecting her. For a young woman, this sort of secrecy was worse than playing with fire. If she was caught with Ilario, *he* could be charged. Misconduct with an unmarried nobleman's daughter had its penalties, if the family so wished to have satisfaction. Unsanctioned as it was, Noemi would also be harshly punished. Some nobles whipped their rebellious daughters into future submission. Others cast them out to fend for themselves or sent them directly to the convent. Noemi knew that even her own friends would not help her in such a situation, too worried that it might tarnish their own prospects. It was a timeless practice; keeping unmarried girls under careful surveillance and in a constant state of resignation until it was decided what to do with them.

When the door opened, firelight flooded through the doorway and covered Noemi in its glow. Smiling reassuringly, Ilario took one of her hands in his and guided her inside, closing the door behind them. Her heart leaping, she thought it might dance away out into the moonlight. This was the first time she'd ever been alone with a man and this wasn't just any man. Their burgeoning love was hallowed in her eyes. How could they hardly know each other, and yet there still be such a deep wanting within her? She only hoped that he would prove to be discreet and careful with her, and that he really did love her, or at least would come to love her from out of those blossoming feelings he'd claimed.

Standing in the rear room on the first floor of his

home, he tenderly led her before the hearth and pulled the hood of her cloak down to rest on her shoulders. For a moment, he stood quietly reviewing her face. And then, reaching to the back of her head, he untied her mask and removing it, sat it upon a small table, a humble slab where he likely took his meals. It was a simple home, the innards rustic and cramped. But she saw that it was tidy and cozy. It smelled divine, just like the pine she'd dreamt of. Removing her cloak entirely, she placed it over a chair. Standing before him in an unadorned brown dress, her ribs felt restrained beneath the cage of her corset, while the soft skin of her bosom rose and fell above the line of her bodice. She was nervous, yet filled with anticipation for what words might be exchanged. Ilario took up one of her hands once more and standing very closely to her, brought it up to his lips where he kissed her fingers. Her hand was dwarfed and delicate within his large and calloused paw.

Even without seeing the rest of his home, she could imagine herself being the mistress of it. Many a day would be spent in this room before the fire. She'd restuff their mattress with fresh and piney smelling sawdust, would prepare appetizing dishes both sweet and savory, and would mend his clothing with careful stitching. Together they would create a happy nest, and fill it with beautiful, healthy children. And though he worked in a prestigious business, and was revered as a maker of gondolas, Ilario wasn't a noble and didn't have to abide by noble rules. His children would be free to marry as they would without having to bow to parental demands. They'd marry for love.

Continuing to hold her hand, he led the way, steering her up a steep wooden stair to the second floor where loft-like was his sleeping chamber. Another fire warmed the space, popping and bright. Shutters over several windows sat open and she could see the full moon without. The room contained another small table, two chairs, a standing washing basin, and a bed. In this room she would hang a mirror, sew soft billowy curtains for the windows, and hang dried flowers and herbs from the rafters for their color and fragrance.

Letting go of his hand, she walked across the floor toward an open door. Peeking within, she found a narrow but airy room facing out over the canal at the front of the house. Another table, covered in papers, and some few chairs. It contained a stairway leading down, straight into his workshop. She imagined that this place would be flooded with sunlight during the day. Ilario clearly tended to his sketches and proposals here. But it would also become a charming nook for her to write letters, stitch, rock her babies, and meet with small company. She could see it all in her mind. Yes, she could be very happy here. But she was getting ahead of herself. Her parents would never permit their union. Even so, she couldn't allow that to ruin this moment.

Retreating to him in the center of his chamber, he invited her to sit before the fire. And so she did. He poured them wine into polished wooden cups. She smiled; normally she drank from pewter or glass. The warmth of the fire and the smell of woodchips from the workshop below were intoxicating, as was the view of that lunar orb just past her reach in the night sky. There they sat, and spoke, and laughed and whispered, for several hours. With every word and look, their hearts drew closer. Their conversation went easily, naturally. And though she was of noble stock and he a craftsman, there was no noticeable difference between them in manner or speech. They were but two Venetians well-suited, enamored, and vastly content.

Mirella

The scene couldn't have been more luxurious. The table end closest to the large hearth in the dining hall had been prepared for two. Places were set with linens in a golden weave, crystal goblets and a glittering wine decanter, with one ambrosial arrangement of flowers. A fine menu had been carefully chosen. Cold salads, spiced meats, roasted vegetables and fresh oysters would be served. For dessert, a platter of chilled fruit, nuts and honeyed delights. The woman herself was in every way exquisite, elegantly dressed and adorned. She'd had to pay extra attention to the planning of such details, especially with two less servants to aid her.

Many would have found the scene garish; certainly it was suspicious. Though it wasn't unheard of for a married noblewoman to entertain important business guests in her husband's absence, official announcements in Mirella's hand officiating Orso's death were about to leave the *palazzo* walls and filter out into the city. After all of the time that had passed since his departure, she was ready to publicly declare that he was no longer with the living.

In making such a claim, Mirella should have been

in mourning and dressed appropriately for it. She should be girding herself for the onslaught of letters that would ensue once Orso's status was made official. She should be tending to her daughters, who in spite of their steely manners, would soon begin to grieve in earnest for their father. But also, there was plague in the city. Despite not knowing how violent the pestilence would become, citizens *all* should have been preparing to cloister themselves within their homes. They should have been ensuring enough food, candles, and firewood were in store; getting ready to brace, should they need to shut off from the world for a pass of time. Rather than sitting to an elaborate feast, Mirella and every other Venetian should have been praying. The servants scurried for the private meal without question, but which of them would dare say anything? None if they wanted to safeguard their place and protection in such a great house.

When all was prepared and Remo's visiting hour was upon her, she shooed the servants from her sight and posed before the fire in wait. At the appointed hour, her guest arrived and was delivered to the inviting scene. The man, now wealthy himself, had donned costly raiment befitting his comfortable place in society. Mirella felt triumphant; he wanted to be pleasing to her eyes as well. Standing before her at the table, he bowed graciously and said her name with warmth and charm. She rose from her place and offered him a delicate hand. He kissed it while peering up into her eyes, prolonging the moment for longer than the greeting usually expected. He was flirting.

Taking in the scene before them, he questioned if this was all for his visit. He had merely requested an audience with her; this was too generous! Would there not be other guests to such a table? Would not her treasured daughters be joining them this evening? Mirella feigned a moment of sorrow, explaining that her neighbors were keeping to their houses because of this recent outbreak, and that her daughters were indisposed and in their rooms, on behalf of their lost father of course. She however, had always understood the value of nurturing the relationships important to her husband's business. When she received Remo's letter asking for a meeting, how could she not comply, for it certainly had something to do with Orso's trade. No?

Two lady servants had reentered, busying themselves around the table, moving as quietly as ghosts, their ears perked to their mistress's every word. One presented a bowl of sweet-smelling water dotted with petals and a clean cloth so that Mirella and her guest could wash their hands before dining. The attendants were both moved by her statement. How considerate their lady was of her husband's affairs, even in spite of the grief she must be keeping at bay. What a strong and dedicated wife.

After the two were seated to table and the wine was poured, Remo's first words were to make a gentle inquiry into whether or not she still hoped for Orso's return. His expressions were caring, his voice empathetic; he too had lost a spouse. She lowered her head. He touched her hand. He could feel her distress. Perhaps this wasn't the best time to discuss business after all? No, Mirella artfully rallied, she was prepared to listen. She smiled sweetly for him, working to draw him in.

She shared how today had been the very first time she'd entered Orso's private place of meeting since he'd gone. Remo nodded with understanding. With so many pressing duties, she hadn't even had the time to begin filtering through her husband's papers. Nevertheless, she was prepared to manage it all on his behalf. Now, what was it that Remo proposed? Of course, she was likely to accept whatever business arrangement he and her husband had been considering. Remo had proved clever in trade. But wait, they should not discuss such matters over dinner! Wouldn't her guest prefer to enjoy the comforts of her table first? There was plenty of time to ponder his proposal after. A look of discomfort flashed over Remo's face, but missed Mirella's notice. She quickly clapped her hands to the servants and the meal commenced.

And so they dined, and drank, and told each other of all that had happened in the years between now and when they'd known each other as youths in Padua. With the comings and goings of the servants tending to them, there wasn't a single word passed that would imply the true nature of their early relationship. Mirella enjoyed this game; and Remo was being such a good actor, disguising his true feelings for her. She laughed pleasantly and often, sometimes reaching out innocently to touch his hand or to offer him some select nibble for his plate. He thanked and complimented her; for her generosity, on how she was just as beautiful as he'd always remembered her, and for how very pleasant her company was on this night. She basked in his words, however carefully he had to arrange them. She appreciated how cautiously he behaved before the keen ears of her attendants. They continued in this way for some hours, and in them, Mirella was reminded of how becoming a man he was.

Finally moving from the table to two comfortable chairs closer to the fire, they carried along their goblets and sat easily while soaking in the warmth and the renewal of friendship that was taking place. But after a short time, Remo guided the conversation back to his proposal. Smiling, Mirella delicately teased him; how eager he was to speak of business! Ah well, persistence was what had given him his successes over the years, and she admired him for it. She was ready to listen.

But what she heard felt like a violent grab to the throat. Remo, having become not only secure but a powerful tradesman with his own wealth, had come to request the hand of Orso and Mirella's daughter, Noemi. When first arriving in *Venezia*, just weeks before he'd met with Orso, Remo had entered a church to pray for the soul of his buried wife. It was there that he'd caught sight of Noemi. She'd lifted her veil to light a candle and he was immediately enraptured. Just outside of the church, he'd employed a random boy to follow the woman and find out which *palazzo* she entered. If the youth returned to Remo's rented apartment with information on her identity, he'd reward him with a gold piece. For a coin of gold, what boy wouldn't run such a simple errand? Remo easily discovered who she was. It was of course, a great surprise to learn of the girl's heritage, but it explained the young lady's great beauty, for he knew firsthand how appealing was her mother! He was determined that Noemi should be his new wife. And visiting Orso, Noemi's father had seemed open to such a connection and had promised to consider it. Unfortunately, Remo had not heard from Orso since that day. This was why he'd written to Mirella. He wanted to reassert his interest in one of the house's noble daughters.

Mirella was uncertain whether or not she could remain civil while acutely experiencing every horrible emotion one would expect with Remo's disclosure. She no longer felt like the lofty and alluring creature that she had believed this man desired just minutes before. How she had deceived herself into believing that his entering their home, under the guise of some business matter, had been to gain access to her! All along, his eyes had been set on one of her children. Perhaps even now, there was something *more* that she didn't know. Had Remo written to Noemi? Had he shared his desires and beguiled her heart? If so, she was a vain, stupid child! Was Remo the man she'd entered that gondola for? Had they *already* met privately, under her very nose?

And why shouldn't Remo want to marry Noemi; the age difference was common in unions. He'd shown himself rich and worthy. Up until just now, *she'd* considered him for herself. She could easily see that this wasn't some twisted plot to pain her, paying her back for leaving him for Orso years ago. They'd both known they could never marry; he was merely the son of one of her father's paid men. Further, even in the midst of their passions, he'd never told her he loved her. She hadn't loved him either.

Even her recent and inexplicable focus on him had been nothing but a bizarre lust, perhaps more so for the contribution he could make to her coffers, rather than for his person. Why had she grappled so quickly for this man? To see how easy it might be to attract Remo once more? How foolish! Her stomach churned and she wished she hadn't dined before hearing this revelation. Quiet reflection would soon settle all of this confusion. Before long, she would banish him from her thoughts forever.

Mirella acted flattered by his interest in her daughter, but quickly informed him of an intended match that she herself had already made for Noemi. A youth named Rodolfo, a son of a powerful house.

Under the burden of such an unpredictable time in her life, and as a loving mother to her children, she would do anything to secure their futures. Mirella believed that this was a very good match for Noemi, that her daughter would be happy. In fact, the signed contract was to arrive at any minute.

"So you see, she is already betrothed." Mirella sighed.

Remo looked strained, trying to keep his displeasure from his hostess. After all, he'd asked for her hand first. He had a prior claim. Mirella disguised her satisfaction over his disappointment, extending more flattery by reminding him of how very desirable a match he'd make for any noble's daughter; just not hers.

The evening ended very differently than she'd imagined. Rather than finding his way into her bed, he'd hastily left the *palazzo*. Mirella considered whether she should go to Noemi's room and smother her with a pillow now, or have her followed so that she could capture these two lovers in the act. Certainly, it *must* have been Remo that Noemi had visited in the night! He'd sought her out, had seduced her after his meeting with Orso. Mirella wasn't jealous, just irate to have been made a fool. She'd have Remo imprisoned if the two were to ever meet again. Now that he'd been told of Noemi's engagement, the law would find any secret meetings particularly damning.

After he had gone, Mirella remained before the fire late into the night, adrift in the winding and angry canals of her thoughts.

Mafalda

She woke to the sound of wood incessantly beating against stone. Sitting up from her hunched over position beneath the dark cloak, a blanket of snow fluttered from off of her body to form a sparkling cloud in the dusky light. Her eyes were swollen and her body incomprehensibly stiff. She wanted to go back to sleep immediately; her body hungered for rest. But then she became aware of a parching thirst and the continual cracking noise, which was overwhelmingly jarring. As she looked around her, she realized that she was touching Venice, her boat smacking marble. Glancing around inside the boat, she saw only one oar.

She'd been so very tired and hadn't even thought she'd make the journey. She kept nodding off as she tried to stroke through the frigid waters. She didn't remember the moment, but the oar must have slipped from her numb fingers and sunk into the depths of the lagoon. She'd given in to the sleep; the urge had been too powerful. And yet, a current, or the waves, or some invisible spirit had pushed her boat onwards. And now she was here. She couldn't think of what to do next. The city was rife with the plague and though she was now immune to it, there were still plenty of other dangers. There was plundering, rape, and murder. Insensible crimes birthed out of greed, fear and madness. The dead, the dying and the desperate, would be found everywhere.

Just a little way down along the platform before her was a crude stairway cut out of the stone. Mafalda moved her hand up to the wall to try and push the boat in the direction of the stair, but with the strength of the tide, the action was useless. Leaning down for the second oar, she used it against the stone, pushing until she met the steps. Freezing mist, briny droplets catching in the wind, blew on her exposed face and hands. Carefully standing, she pressed one hand on the stone for support, the marble like ice to the touch, and stepped overboard. As she teetered on the bottom step just above the water, she believed her swollen feet might burst out of her pilfered slippers. They throbbed and burned at the bottom of legs that she alarmingly could hardly feel. But in spite of her physical plight, she still felt the miracle that it was to be standing in Venice once more. She was climbing the stairs to Heaven after escaping through the gates of Hell.

Carefully ascending to the top, she scanned the vacant marble pathway and buildings, shocked to discover that she knew exactly where she was. A short stumble would bring her to the home of Aurelia the courtesan. More importantly, it was also the residence of another courtesan to have entered the profession, Fina. Mafalda had accompanied her sister on visits there when Aurelia's family was still alive. She'd heard that the innards of the home had been substantially improved upon since their deaths, owing to Aurelia's quickly securing two vastly rich patrons in succession. Not only had such luck increased her wealth, but it had also sparked her reputation as a promising courtesan.

Mafalda couldn't blame Fina for following in her friend's footsteps. She'd fled the House of Orso the very night that their mother had informed them of the decision to send them to the convent. It took Mirella several days to learn where she'd gone, even though she'd guessed rightly. Aurelia ignored two missives by their mother, demands to reveal whether or not Fina was under her roof. Their mother would likely have hunted her out in person if the plague hadn't been afoot. Fina finally returned word herself however, naming herself a courtesan.

The very next morning after Fina walked boldly out to make her own way, Mafalda found herself a prisoner. Paola too, had been locked inside her own chamber, or so disclosed a temporary handmaiden obtained from a neighboring *palazzo*. Mirella didn't want to chance any more daughters absconding in the dead of night, and so she locked them in. Everything was already getting out of control and the reputation of the House of Orso would begin to suffer for it, especially because it wasn't just *one* child who had escaped, but also Mirella's prized marriageable gem. Noemi had also disappeared, on the same night as Fina. Mafalda had no idea where she might have gone; the news had baffled her.

The borrowed servant had been called for to help with the labor on account of Tonia and Martinella's untimely passing. Mafalda had passed this lady several times in the local *campo*. She looked to be about 25, but she knew nothing else about her. Zeta was plain but very pretty; she had brown hair and eyes, clean smooth skin, and the finest white teeth. After getting a closer look, Mafalda believed that had she been born a noble lady with an easy life and a sumptuous closet at her disposal, word of her beauty would have circulated. She'd seen the new servant buzzing about her duties, but only spoke to her after being confined to her room.

Mirella had the key to her door and locked it from the outside, only admitting Zeta to bring meals and attend to the chores of the room. Mirella would make way for the servant and then shut her in, but always returned within half an hour to let her out again. It was from Zeta, who was neither gossipy nor intolerably mute, that Mafalda learned of all that was astir. It was now nearly a week and Noemi hadn't returned. There wasn't even a hint as to where she had gone. Had their mother any private guess? All that was known was that Noemi had hastily snatched up some possessions, leaving her room in disorder.

It was now certain that a wedding would not take place. But neither was it because of Noemi's now soiled name, nor the scourge spreading through the city. Rodolfo had been found stabbed to death in a shadowy street not at all far away. It was thought that he'd met with a prowler on the street while walking home after a night of drinking and whoring. He'd been killed the same night Noemi had left.

The news had been more shocking than if she'd learned that Rodolfo had caught the plague. For his mean reputation and entitled behavior, Mafalda had disliked him as an arrogant cur. It certainly would have been torture for Noemi if the wedding had taken place. However, a stabbing was an exceptionally cruel way to die. His death was the result of plague-related turbulence, and it was sobering.

She also learned from Zeta, that Mirella would have her two remaining daughters enclosed as immediately as possible. After all that had transpired, she was eager to deliver them to their cells and have it settled. Once all her children were gone from her, Mafalda guessed that her mother would publicly disown her sisters. Noemi *might* have run off with a man, and Fina was about to entertain a great many of them. Neither of them would ever be admitted into the House of Orso again.

Watching seagulls squall as they dove through the sky above her window, Mafalda felt sad for their mother. She'd only been making the same arrangements any other noble parent would have made, and yet two of her daughters had irrevocably rebelled. One of these precious children remained unaccounted for. There was also the alleged death of their esteemed father. Brokenhearted, Mirella now had the heavy burden of managing all that he had left behind. And then there was the plague, which would have caused a mother great worry. Though Mirella had never been affectionate, Mafalda would always love her. All the sorrow she felt however, weighed far greater for herself and for each of her sisters, each flung out on their own path to destiny.

Dejected as she surveilled the quiet square below, Mafalda began to cry. Zeta nervously scraped the spent ashes from out of her small fireplace, remaining silent. Everything was in chaos, and soon she'd have eternal reason for tears while tucked away in a nunnery. Her life would be over, just when it had begun. It was through those tears that she'd spied the neighbor woman and her confrontation with the *beccamorto*. In minutes, the dreg was to be run through with a sword. Witnessing such a ghastly scene, she began to feel a far darker despair creeping in. The Black Death was near; she could see it from her window. Even in a nunnery, there would be no safe place to hide, from the plague or from violence. Knowing this, she felt terrified and alone.

Zeta stood up with a start, ashes swirling about her skirts. She could hear the screaming filtering up and in through the window. Men were also shouting in alarm. The servant woman's eyes were full and round with attention; she too was afraid.

Noemi

Swiftly as she could manage, Noemi reviewed her possessions and considered what would be most important to take with her. In fleeing from her home this night, she knew that anything could happen. She prayed that Ilario would shelter her, prayed that he might even ask her to remain with him always. The hopes of securing his eternal protection made her blind to the risks she was taking in leaving her family. But what else could she do? Allow her own enslavement to Rodolfo? For all of his wealth, he'd never be able to offer her the humble things she desired in life: respect, tenderness, and love.

She was certain that they couldn't hide in Ilario's workshop for very long before one of the neighbors noticed her, making way for her mother to learn of her whereabouts. At the first notice of her absence, Mirella would be furious. She was just the sort too, to press charges against Ilario in the courts and teach Noemi a lesson for her disobedience. Still, running away was the only way to take control of her future. However, she needed to take what jewels and coins she could carry. Especially since there *was* the possibility that Ilario would eschew her. Any man of good reputation, however much in love, would be putting his neck out to marry under such circumstances. It could ruin Ilario's business, and how could a gondola maker survive in any place but Venice? Could she bear the guilt of taking away his beloved trade?

Even with all of these unknowns, a far greater threat hung over them. The plague; they might survive it, they might not. Noemi's breast heaved with worry as she made haste, heaping a small fortune worth of pearls, gems and coins into a large square of embroidered cloth, wrapping the contents up tightly.

After nightfall, Noemi covered herself in a warm cloak and stuffed her belongings into the pockets of her garments. The cloak pulled heavily to one side, hanging with the weight of hidden treasures. Scanning around her chamber, the very room where she'd slumbered her entire life, she said goodbye. It was possible that she would never see it again. Quietly peeking out her door, she found the hallway free from anyone. Toeing out, she had to pause and hide in dark corners more than once, alerted by the sound of steps and hurrying servants. The quickest way out took her past one of several massive stone doorways that led into the dining hall. As she dashed past in the shadows, warm firelight flickered in her pathway. So did the sounds of merriment, a man's and a woman's mirth. Her mother was entertaining. Noemi didn't recognize his voice, and only hoped that she hadn't been spotted as she ran past. The sound of her mother's vivacious laughter made her sad. What if tonight was the last time she ever heard it?

She eventually made her way through the house and slipped out of a street-side door. As she stood below the archway, ready to make her escape, she was given a fright. The stone *calle* was quiet, apart from a faint jingling and the creaking of wheels. Too wary to peek out and see who was coming, she pulled down her dark hood and backed up as far into the hollow of the doorway as she could. Whoever was coming would pass, and then she could set out. She worked to breath as little as possible, as the temperature had turned frigid and her exhalations were visibly cloudy; it was now winter in Venice.

Noemi knew the creaking of wagon wheels, but this lane was far too thin for one to make its way down. Whatever was coming, it made a sound that was similar. What was that jingle, such as a set of bells? It didn't take long before she saw the *beccamorto* advancing with a narrow pull wagon, his body trudging along between two poles to haul it. Around one of his ankles was tied a strand of bells, to announce that he was in the neighborhood should anyone need to bring out their dead. And in the wagon even now, two bodies, those of a woman and a little boy. Were they from the same family, mother and child? As the wagon bumbled along over the uneven stones in the *calle*, it tilted and shook and the bruised bodies shifted gruesomely. A putrid smell wafted into Noemi's hiding spot as they passed and she threw her hand up over her nose and mouth. In but a moment the horrible sight had passed, but Noemi had now seen the truth of the scourge. These were the first plague victims she'd ever beheld. What if even their deathly odor could pass on the infection? But that was nonsense; no *beccamorto* could ever live out a single day if this was true, so smothered by the scent of plague.

Frantically making the sign of the cross over herself, she bounded out of the doorway and fled in the opposite direction. If she ran fast enough, perhaps she could make it to Ilario before quarter of an hour had passed. As she made her way, she quickly realized that she'd made one serious mistake. She'd gone out of the house without the disguise of a mask. It was incomprehensible that she could have forgotten such an important cover; she'd been wearing a mask or veil out upon the streets since *birth*. Exposed, anyone that she encountered in the scant minutes it took her to reach Ilario, could identify her. And someone did.

At an intersection of thin lanes just minutes from the *palazzo*, a man stumbled out before her from one direction, just as she was hastily running in another. Their bodies met and they both nearly fell from the sudden impact. Surprised, she tried to turn her face away as she reeled, and then attempted to sprint past the man before he could catch his balance. The glimpse she'd caught of him indicated that he was a noble, finely dressed, yet like her, was missing the cover of a mask. She could smell rancid wine and sweat. As she moved to slip past him while he was not yet fully standing again, he caught her wrist firmly.

"Nomeeeiii?" The man slurred in his drunkenness. His condition did not hamper his strength; he had a tight grip on her. She tried to keep from facing him and tugged her arm hard to get away. But sensing her struggle against him, he pulled her back forcefully and they met face-to-face. It was Rodolfo.

Paola

Perhaps she'd go mad. She'd heard of other girls doing so, she might too. Sleeping had already been poor while she was ill, but trying to sleep in her room ever since she'd found Martinella expired before her in her chair proved futile. Though it had been an accidental death, and though Martinella couldn't have suffered much with the infection taking her so quickly, it felt impossible that she'd ever reconcile with the loss of a beloved friend by such ordinary means. A cut to the hand; life was far too fragile. It drove her to tears. And then there was Tonia, who'd gone unnaturally. It plagued Paola's thoughts to remember the maiden's terrible expression, and the fistful of her own candies. The drops were poisoned, and Paola had come to possess them by her mother. Why would Mirella intentionally work to poison her own daughter? What had Paola done to displease her so wholly, that Mirella would risk her own immortal soul by killing her child? It made no sense at all, but she and Fina had been so disturbed by the idea, that they'd kept the discovery of the confections a secret. It was causing her enough fear to make her brain crack. And now she was locked in her room, paranoid of every tray of food that the new servant, Zeta, was bringing her. What if her mother tried to accomplish what she'd set out to do by dousing her soup with poison? Or perhaps she might drip it liberally into her wine, without anyone's notice. Or just as disturbing, she might have bribed Zeta to do it!

Paola hadn't been able to bring herself to eat very much since she'd been closed up in her chamber. Since she couldn't filch it from the kitchen herself, she was nervous to put it in her mouth. She wished she could have even just one of her sisters with her now. The roomy place felt as though it would close in on her, and at night, she dreaded the possible sight of Martinella or Tonia; what if they came to haunt her? She paced the room. When would she be going to the nunnery? Why was it necessary to keep her locked up? Who was this servant that she didn't know and didn't trust? But the very worst question of all was, why had her mother wanted her dead?

After being locked within for nearly a week, Zeta came to inform her that Mirella was sending her to the nunnery that very day. Mafalda would join her there soon, but not today, for Mirella wasn't about to ride in a gondola with both of them at the same time. She needed to keep a good watch over them individually, to ensure that neither ran away. Paola couldn't understand why she couldn't go with Mafalda. Why were they being punished so severely for what Fina and Noemi had chosen to do?

Paola was now to leave the outside world for a life of enclosure without anyone's hand to hold, and she felt no courage. She felt something close to terror at the thought of climbing into a vessel with her mother. Dread swirled around her. What if Mirella was lying to her? What if she wasn't taking her to the convent at all, but planned to dispose of her in the lagoon like a sack of unwanted kittens? If only she could wake up to discover her fears were all unfounded, but the taste from those lemony, poisonous sweets remained tart upon her tongue.

With a grumbling and anxious stomach, she prepared as best she could. The nuns had very strict rules; keeping showy and expensive personal possessions was not permitted. What would happen to her beloved things? Who would wear her pretty clothes and decorate themselves with this precious jewelry? What would happen to all of the gifts she'd been given by her family? What had they ever mattered, those wondrous things that she'd collected from the market, if she was not allowed to take any of them with her? Worse still, at only 15 and if she were to live a long life, how would she endure it without any beautiful and comfortable things? Paola thought about Tonia, how she'd stolen some of her treasures; she immediately forgave her. The theft wasn't right, but Tonia had only wanted something pleasing in her onerous world. Paola would soon be in the same predicament. She thought of Zeta then too, and felt ashamed that she'd been so wary of her in spite of how kind the young woman was treating her.

Laying out a piece of paper, she sat to her writing table. With the spectacular quill plucked from a Chinese Golden Pheasant, she wrote out a list of items, bestowing her small valuables to the remaining servants in the *palazzo*, even an opal ring to Zeta. Taking up a small chest, she gathered the items into it and placed the letter within. The signed document would make it impermissible for her mother to use her belongings in any other way. That was, unless she burned the signed paper. Mirella was capable of hurting her own daughter; she'd exact lesser offenses as well. Paola would deliver the casket to Zeta directly and trust her to be honorable enough to distribute the riches.

When next the attendant returned to her chamber, Paola was feeling weak in body but calm in mind. Zeta was there to prepare her for her last gondola ride through Venice.

"Kind lady..." Paola started, her face pale and angelic, surrounded by her dark hair.

"Yes, mistress?" Zeta looked surprised. Paola had hardly spoken a word to her since she'd been summoned from the next noble house.

"Is that wine there in that vessel safe for me to drink?" She queried while staring directly into Zeta's eyes. She stood tall, seeking the truth. Paola's youthful innocence was leaving her. Even after a short time in enclosure, she was certain to become an impenetrable rock.

"Safe?" Zeta asked, confused.

"*Come* Zeta, the servants of this house gossip as much as they do in every other. You are also our neighbor. You *know* that I was recently made ill by poison." She returned curtly, though with the softness of someone lacking energy.

"Yes Paola, I know. But it was Tonia who sinned against you, and now she is days buried. Of whom should you be afraid? Who else would taint your wine?" Zeta spoke sincerely, even glancing around the room with a hint of paranoia. It was clear that Mirella hadn't bribed her.

Paola filled a goblet full and gulped, soon filling it again and doing the same. She was very thirsty. She'd need some strength in case her mother made any sudden moves along their brief passage.

"Zeta...that box there." Paola spoke as she swirled her nearly empty chalice and stared off toward the window without expression. "My treasures are within. Soon a nun, I cannot take them with me. You are the only one that I can entrust it to; you may be the last person I see here in this house." She turned to look at Zeta once more. "You'll find a parchment in the chest. The *very* hour that I leave, please disperse the items as it is written. There is a ring inside for you. I cherished the band and hope you will keep it. But do not hesitate to sell it if you ever must. And this, take this as well."

Returning to the writing desk, she set down the goblet and picked up her quill. The rainbow colors were spectacular, like the beautiful life Paola would forever dream of but never experience.

"I do not know how to write, Mistress Paola." There was a sad look on the servant's face. Despite not knowing this esteemed daughter well, it was hard for Zeta to watch such a frail and noble creature forced into exile. For how many centuries, and for how many noble ladies, had this scene played out in other houses?

How many parents locked their rebellious daughters into their chambers, waiting to secure them wherever was planned? Zeta knew this girl wasn't rebellious; she had her sisters to blame for her captivity.

"Why not learn to?" A hopeful smile moved upon Paola's lips. "Be my friend, and we can exchange missives. I have no friends, besides my sisters. You could tell me of the world outside. Though I am noble born, you are *free* and so have the better end of things. For such a gift of words, the luxury of news, I would be beholden to you."

Paola was genuine. She knew that she would yearn for letters, for just a page describing news of Venice. To but read of the festivals and of the food, to catch but a windy word about the weather or a mention of the sea. To but even share in another woman's life; her marriage and her births, toiling in a life that was true.

Zeta knew that she could make no promise. There was no time for learning, and no one to teach her. Further, Venice was shaking up harder and harder with each passing moment, and everyone's future was unknown.

"Thank you good lady, for your kindnesses, for myself and for the others too." Zeta reached out to accept the offering and twirled the plume. A dab of ink still wet on its nib blackened some of her fingers. She wiped them nervously upon her apron. After a pause, though she felt pained to have to utter the words, she forced herself, for she was under orders. "We must prepare now mistress. Your time is at hand."

Mafalda

It was getting dark as she banged on one of the doors, having first covered her frozen hand with her cloak to try and avoid the sting she'd feel when her hand met the hard wood; *that* hand, still sticky and morbid-looking following the bloody fray with the *beccamorto*. She banged as hard as she could, having little strength; she found the sound of her knocking pathetically dull. Who would hear her? She was too weak to raise her voice and hope to be heard by a servant.

Mafalda hadn't encountered anyone along her short walk. Glancing around her, she quickly tried the door to see if it was unlocked. It wasn't. But of course no one would ever leave a door open during these hellish days; what with vandals, infection, and those gone insane from their losses who were now out wandering in the streets. It was strange that there wasn't a single soul rushing here or there along the *calle*. The city was disturbingly quiet, not even a distant scream.

Unexpectedly, the silence began to fill her with panic. She had to get inside the house and get warm; she had to get off of the street. She could feel death coming for her from around the next corner; she had yet to escape it! She would expire right here in the doorway. This was the reason why everything was so quiet; death was *everywhere*. A prickly anxiety flooded her bosom and her heart raced. She hadn't even felt such intense dread on the brink of killing that man, nor even when she believed it could be a beloved sister dead and lying facedown in the boat. Was this her body awakening after a numbing shock? Or were her senses sending her one last and final warning that she *would* die if she didn't get warm?

Scurrying to the next door like a desperate rat, she found it also secure. She banged, but there was no reply. If there was someone inside, they may not even answer the door for fear of what might be without. It was difficult to move fast, but she had to, slipping along the outside of the *palazzo* until she was on a thin lane that faced the dwelling's canal. The day was quickly turning into night. In the dimming light, she could see someone boating toward the house not very far away. Two people were in the craft, wearing dark raiment and gliding fast along the water. Mafalda felt the urgency to hide. There wasn't enough time to get to the waterside door before the boat passed and it was certain to be locked, so she hurried under the portico that led into the boat dock. Several fine gondolas were moored below the building. She stood tall and flat against the stone wall nearest where the boat was approaching from; they might pass without noticing her in the shadows. The necessity for caution felt cruel in her present circumstances. She so desperately needed help, but it was too risky. During the plague, even good people were not themselves.

Standing as horizontal as she could, she tried to temper her breath for fear that the strangers would see her vapors in the cold. As the vessel came nearer and nearer, she could hear the familiar sound of paddling and the lapping of water at the sides of the boat as it cut along. She thought her heart might fail, housed in such a brittle cage. If these men were criminals, she would be unable to fight them off. As the craft floated smoothly into view of her concealed position, Mafalda couldn't believe her eyes. It was Baldovino and his father, Santino.

Her voice broke with emotion as she called out to them. "Baldovino! Baldovino and Santino! 'Tis Mafalda! Here, here I am. *Fermo*, stop!"

The men, who were sitting in the boat and on their guard as much as Mafalda, looked surprised and serious to hear their own names being called out.

When they saw her, Baldovino who manned the craft hurried to manage the oar and slow the boat. Soon it was moving in reverse, and backing into the covered refuge.

"Mafalda? How do we know you mistress?" Croaked Santino.

The elder man looked far more aged than she remembered him being when she'd met him delivering oysters to the kitchen. He'd clearly forgotten her, but in these times stress could muddle memories. Baldovino too, appeared tired and worn, but he remained more sharply handsome than any man in her memory. She knew that she had to be a horror to his eyes, sickly and beaten.

"Are you well, friends?" Mafalda asked, slowly creeping out from her hiding spot as though dangers still lurked. She tried to keep her voice low, searching Baldovino's face.

"We are mistress, we are whole. Father, this is Mafalda of the House of Orso." Baldovino stated slowly without removing his eyes from her.

Whole and healthy while she was hideous, yet Baldovino's expression was warm and full of concern. Tears began to well in her eyes to glimpse a look of tenderness.

"Ah yes! The keeper of your house, Martinella...does she fare well? We have not been about our deliveries, but I guess you know that few men are." Santino bumbled sullenly.

Mafalda could do nothing but tell the truth. "I am sorry to say, good sir, Martinella has died. But in her sleep, Santino. Not of the plague."

She thought that it was strange that he should ask about their mutual friend, even one so dear as Martinella. Wasn't he shocked by her deathly appearance? He rather should have gasped and said nothing. Santino nodded solemnly while keeping his eyes averted, the peppery hairs on his face unshaven for days and his hair disheveled. He was pale too. Mafalda sensed just then that he might not be so whole in mind.

"We too have lost..." Santino mumbled while gazing over the water, "...we too."

If the meeting had been under better circumstances, she would have coaxed out and comforted their sorrows. Presently however, she was more in need than they.

"Mafalda...the sickness?" Baldovino whispered it cautiously and gently.

"Yes. I am come up from the grave." He couldn't

know how literal those words were. "By some miracle, I have survived. Do you know this house?" She asked, looking up at the stones above her head and then back at him.

"I am unfamiliar with it." His voice cracked, pained to see that she'd been so very ill.

"This is the House of Aurelia." She tried hard not to cry. "My sister Fina has become a courtesan and has taken up residence here. No one is answering the door. As you can see, I need a fire, food and sleep. I would not ask that you come too close to me, in case the pestilence lingers still. But, if you could break the lock, so that I can take refuge inside?"

"Yes. Of course." He uttered, quickly standing.

Santino took the oar from his son and sat patiently. He glanced up and smiled at Mafalda. Though kind, the look was disquieting. Whatever they had been through was shining through in his eyes. The man needed rest. Climbing a stone step up to platform level, Baldovino approached the waterside portal to the home. Mafalda hovered safely away while he worked. With the same dagger he used to shuck oysters, he wedged the tip into the keyhole and fiddled. After some moments, there was a clink, and then a creak as he pushed the door open inwardly by several inches.

She let out a small sigh of relief.

Still keeping her distance, yet advancing close enough for him alone to hear her, she thanked him. Her head fell, hanging down while soft tears began to drop from her eyes. She felt that she might collapse from the drowsiness that was once again becoming unbearable. She wished that she could hug him, press into his warm body and fall asleep there. She raised her head with difficulty.

"Take heart, gentle bird. You are *alive*. Go within and seek rest." He paused, glancing at his father sitting in a quiet reverie in the boat. Looking back again, his expression now reflected deep pain. "I would stay with you Mafalda. Or, or I would take you with us. But it cannot be so."

She noticed then that his eyes had moved to her breast. The sullied cloak had slipped down, leaving some of her skin exposed where thin cotton did not cover. The gold chain and pearl had worked their way out over the sheer fabric.

When his eyes shifted back to look into her own, it was the same as in the dream with her sisters all around her. That moment, when Fina had looked into her eyes and had urged her to wake, Mafalda had not heard the words. She had only felt them. At this moment, it was the same. Baldovino had said that he loved her. She loved him too. She didn't want him to ever leave her side. She wanted him to stay. But there was more in the message that passed between them. He had also said goodbye.

"Go in now mistress." He spoke aloud. "Go in. Get thee rest, and *live*." A hopeful smile appeared on his lips, but quickly slipped away. He then pivoted, retreating to the boat.

As Mafalda clutched at the oyster's seed hanging from her neck, she found his going oddly fluid. What a strange thing her body's strain was doing to her eyes. Baldovino was floating fast above the stones. She blinked hard and turned away. She could not watch him go, could not meet his gaze as he boated back out and away down the canal. Quietly, she entered the *palazzo*, whispering her own goodbye as tears continued to fall upon her cheeks. And though the door had been forced for lack of anyone's answer to the knocking, she remained wary. No one there to greet her didn't mean there was no one yet inside.

Mirella

She spied Paola standing by the window when she unlocked the chamber door. The girl had been warned to remove any finery that she wore, even the delicate fabrics that were her underclothing. They were to be traded in for the coarser threads she'd soon become accustomed to. Paola donned a dark cotton dress and her raven hair was bound in a low knot above her neck. A thick mantle of rough grey wool waited upon a chair for her journey. It would scratch the neck but keep out the cold.

Busying herself removing linens from Paola's bed, Zeta looked uncomfortable. As Paola turned toward her mother, she wore a blank look and her features were as pale as ever. The servant hurried over to her, snatching up the winter cloak. After the mantle was in place, Zeta made an awkward fuss while reviewing the noble girl's readiness. Soon she squeezed her hand.

"Have courage, Paola." She whispered with a smile. The youth smiled back weakly and then walked straight ahead toward the door while avoiding her mother's gaze.

Stepping out waterside, a gondolier was found waiting in one of the family's glossy vessels. The gondola supported a small private cabin, but Paola refused to get into the boat following her mother's direction.

"No. I will sit in the open. I wish to see the city." She said.

Mirella waved to the boatman who retired the gondola for another with airy seating. Mirella would have preferred a *felze* to harbor them from the cold; the canals in winter were especially chilling, even if dressed very warmly. However, she hadn't the energy to argue.

As they careened through the canals, Paola reviewed every building and walkway that they passed, while inhaling as much air as she could fit into her modest lungs. Mirella could see that her daughter was saying goodbye. Though the convent was in Venice, once within its walls, Paola would never step out again.

The streets were quiet and only a few people scurried here and there; the encroaching plague was keeping people to their houses. However, one man walked in full view of the canal, catching both of their notice. He wore a long black garment with billowy sleeves and a black hood, his face covered with a mask. It wasn't just any disguise; it was the bird-like mask of a plague doctor. The alarming realization that the pestilence was really here, taking lives in these winding *calli*, made Mirella shudder. As they floated by, he turned his face in their direction, the eye slits of the mask covered in black linen, the beak undeniably stuffed with purifying herbs. Mirella looked away; what if he had to be summoned to the House of Orso? What if she fell ill and that face looked down at her as she lay in her bed? She needed to make haste in also getting Mafalda to the nunnery, and in directing the servants with stocking the larder. After that, they would bolt the doors and wait. There was always the option of fleeing the city; surely many other nobles already had. But that was no guarantee that they wouldn't encounter the plague on *terra firma*. They weren't safe anywhere.

With that grim thought, she glanced back at her daughter who was now looking straight at her. Her heart jumped when she saw her face. In that moment, how bizarrely it looked so like the face of her sister Lagia, when they were yet young women. She felt pained and missed her then.

Paola spoke firmly. "Shall I suffer *three* deaths mother? First your poison, next confinement, and then the plague?"

Mirella's eyes grew large with her daughter's

words and her breath momentarily caught in her throat. She brought her hand up to her mouth in surprise. Not only did Paola look so much like Lagia just then, but she had also eerily uttered the very fate Lagia had succumb to. Of course, Lagia had not been *poisoned*. But Mirella's stealing Orso from her had likely delivered similar symptoms.

"What surprises you about my question? Isn't it true?" No girlish plea could be found on Paola's face, instead was something cold and intimidating. Mirella couldn't shake how much she reminded her of her wronged sister. She could only understand the manifestation as coming from her discomfort in seeing the plague doctor, and perhaps some suppressed guilt over Lagia's fate. Mirella was more tired and anxious than she'd believed.

Clearing her throat, she chided her daughter with a gentle smile, "Poison? What poison child? You call being chosen for the nunnery *poison*? All girls, noble yet unsuitable for marriage, must go to the convent Paola. It is your *duty* to your parents." She tried to keep her breathing steady, but she felt alarmingly dismantled.

"Unsuitable? None of us are *unsuitable*. Parents, you say? Father is gone now!" Paola whimpered angrily while solemnly making the sign of the cross over her body. "I have no brothers, which means everything that was father's goes to *you*. Why not allow us to marry? Cannot you spare a little gold to arrange our dowries? Are you planning to marry again? To have a son? Must you keep it all for yourself? Cannot you let us be *free*? Cannot you grant us a chance for happiness! A chance for love, as you and father had?" Paola's eyes were large and glossy, a hint of her youthful emotions had returned to her. This was her one last chance to speak to her mother's heart.

"I will hear none of this Paola. It is the way things *are*." Mirella replied, keeping control over her voice in spite of the burgeoning guilt her daughter was drawing out.

Yes, Mirella had desired Remo, might have even married him. And it was true that should they have been *able* to bear sons, the firstborn of them would have inherited all by law. But the fact was, sending her daughters to the nunnery wasn't about succession any more than it was about a Venetian tradition. It was about something *else*.

"Did you try to hurt me, mother? Was it *you* who tried to poison me?" Paola was throwing all caution over the side of the boat. She wanted to know the truth.

"*Paola*, you know very well what Tonia did. She stole from you! She was a jealous heathen! She slipped you the juice of nightshade berries. Enough of *this*." She hissed with a squint of her eyes and a disbelieving nod of her head.

Paola turned away, her chest rising and falling heavily. She sat mute the rest of the way, as did Mirella. Soon standing before the convent door, Mirella banged hard with a brass knocker upon the head of a lion with wings around it. It was a symbol of Venice's patron saint, St. Mark. For a long moment, all was silent until a small slit covered by a metal plate shifted open and two beady eyes peered out.

"Yes?" Asked the eyes' voice sharply.

"This is Paola, daughter of the House of Orso. Our arrangement for her is to commence today." Mirella explained with a forced smile on her face.

"And so it is." Replied the nun. "And has the plague been in your house, wife of Orso?"

"No." She replied.

"Very well." And with that, the nun unbolted the door to allow the girl to enter.

Paola turned to her mother and face-to-face seethed, "It was in the *sweets* that you gave me, tart with lemon and sour with poison! Tonia stole some from my room and ate too many. It was *you*. Repent of your lies and selfishness, before such a poison makes its way back to you. Before *the plague* finds you. It's coming!"

Confusion and horror coursed through Mirella's body as her daughter slipped away and disappeared into the cavernous shadows past the doorway. The nun quickly shut the portal and slid the plate closed. Hurried footsteps could be heard trailing away into the nunnery.

The lemon confections; she had nearly forgotten about those. Mirella *had* given them to Paola, but they had originally come from Orso. Those sweets had been meant for *her*!

Mafalda

Mafalda closed the door behind her and with a bolt at the top of it, locked herself in. She couldn't chance leaving the door ajar for someone else to enter. Making her way down a long hallway, she encountered no one. It was drafty and dim. Clearly, no servants were keeping the place lit, a necessity during the day in many cavernous parts of a *palazzo*. But at least she was safely inside and not *out there*. Peering into various ground-level rooms as she went, they were all the same. Empty, barren of people, and dark. She was nervous, though the feeling was different from when she had been out on the *calle*. What if she were to find someone sick and abandoned, or worse, bodies that had yielded? What if she found Fina's? It was only natural to think of this; it was after all, possible. Eventually, she staggered into a mighty kitchen not unlike the one in her own home. For an instant, she thought again of Baldovino and of the day they'd met in that kitchen.

Looking around, she found that the hearth, though not a blazing fire, had a layer of red embers smoldering at its floor! But there was no one here either. Thankfully, she didn't sense any signs of upheaval. There was no hint of the plague; no proof that anyone had prepared to doctor the sick from out of this kitchen. There were no bloody rags or soiled washbasins, no bottles of unguents or small sacks of clarifying herbs.

The kitchen in any noble house was always a highly trafficked room, and no good servant would dare to let a healthy fire run out. Whether winter or summer, it was necessary for cooking, and hot water was needed all day long. So where were they? If she'd cried out, she would have heard an echo. She spotted a brass pitcher on one long shelf and shimmied over to it. Grasping for it and peering in, she then lifted it to her nose for a sniff. It was souring wine. She would have preferred water, but this was a start. Tilting it to her face, she gulped back enough to satisfy her for the moment. Too much and her shocked system would only vomit it back up. It burned her throat as it went down, and twisted her stomach.

Going out, she pulled herself up a grand marble stair. She discovered all the chamber doors open, and other various places in the same empty manner. She was too exhausted to search the rooms in any great detail, and only glanced in for signs of another human. There was no one. There were embers still glowing in two bedrooms however, and she knew to whom they must belong. The first, Aurelia's with its fine décor and plush furnishings. How fine a chamber! Mafalda had never been in any of the bedchambers on any previous visits, only the great room toward the front of the house on the first floor. There the girls had gossiped and sat stitching while large high windows let the light flood in. The house had been far shabbier then. The second room was certainly Fina's. Mafalda instantly recognized one of her gowns rumpled and thrown out over the bed.

With the glowing embers in three of the fires and not more, she could very well paint the scene. The servants had scattered to wherever they would, on account of the terrifying news of the plague. They'd left their two courtesan mistresses to fend for themselves. And with some dishevelment of the bedchambers, the ladies too must have decided to leave. They'd packed up in a hurry it seemed, perhaps even just this morning. Mafalda had missed her sister by just one day of hours. She wondered where the women had gone. Maybe they'd left Venice altogether.

She closed herself up into Fina's room. If she could get the fire going again, the room would build some heat and she could sleep. Removing the cloak she'd taken from the dead woman at the circumference of the pit, she walked up to the large fireplace and carefully placed it over the coals. Instantly the cloak began to smolder, soon bursting into flames. Though inviting to her face, her hands ached before the fire when the heat touched them. In thawing her frozen limbs, it was almost certain there would be some permanent damage. Some injured nerves and pain. An unpleasant thought rose in her mind. What if the icy damage was worse than that? But only time would tell.

Taking advantage of the burning mantle, she took a few quartered logs from a pile aside the fireplace and carefully stoked the fire until the wood caught. She was so thankful for the embers. It had only taken a few minutes to build up a fire that might have taken half an hour longer to start. She might have given up, for she had so little energy within her. Would have crawled into Fina's bed and shivered. Heat began to emanate from the fireplace, spreading out into the chamber. With the cloak removed, and standing before the flames in only her thin shift, Mafalda began to smell herself as she thawed. She stank. Like the pungent blood still coloring one of her hands in a splotchy glove, it was a metallic, fearsome smell. There was the remnant scent of death, which clung to her after having lain with corpses. Further still, the stink of her illness, the unwashed sweat that had carried out her infection. All coalesced, the result was unbearable. Had Baldovino smelled her wretchedness? He'd definitely *seen* her. She was too sick and dejected to seek out a mirror. But if she had one easily before her, she would have lost all courage.

A ceramic washbasin sat tall on an ornately carved wooden stand. Within, there was a pool of chilly, milky water and aside it, a small slice of soap and a damp rag. Her sister had lately washed, not bothering to discard the sullied water before she left. The dirtied water was more than good enough for Mafalda; it was a godsend. The basin being not very large, she picked up the bowl and rag and careful not to spill the contents, moved it over to the fire. Sitting it before the hearth, she removed her damp and frozen gown and threw it upon the fire. It smoked and let off a smell that would scare a child to death; she gagged. Kicking off the slippers she'd taken from yet another dead woman, she tossed them in too. It was all contaminated and soiled beyond repair; the garments must burn. Better to do it now before they introduced the pestilence into the room, to say nothing that *she* might still be contagious.

Mafalda knew that she would have to burn Fina's

bedcovers once she recovered. But first, she was going to sleep in that bed for a long, long time. Naked, she placed several more logs on the fire, and then kneeled down by the basin. The water wasn't yet warm, but she could wait no longer. She washed herself as best she could, as closely to the fire as she could get, her body filled with tremors from the cold and shock.

When she was done, she stared into the foul basin with disgust. Blood, dirt, sweat, pus, and death. She moved it away to sit beside the door, spreading the filthy cloth over its top. She quickly found some of her sister's fresh under gowns, folded neatly in a chest. She put on two, layering one atop the other for warmth. Feebly, she then got into bed, pulling up all the thick covers to nest her. She was thankful for the warm winter blankets, and for one very soft fur. And though she ached, hungered and thirsted, under their heavy comfort, she slept.

Noemi

She was horrified to be caught up by the very man her mother had attempted to marry her to. She'd been kind enough to him in their home at her mother's insistence, despite his hideous insensitivities and demanding nature. Idleness and wealth were a bad combination; he was as unforgivably selfish as his tongue was sharp. She couldn't imagine becoming his wife. Certainly, he'd been polite when hosted. But she could sense the true realities of his personality; he was the sort to spit on a beggar and beat a harlot. He'd strike a wife too, and criticize her imperfections unceasingly. Noemi was certain of it. That was the sort of entertainments men of his kind enjoyed.

The very way he was gripping her wrist caused her pain. Even though she was out alone, late at night, so very compromising for a noble Venetian woman, and even though she was to be engaged to him and her outing looked very bad for a future wife, his hold on her was not the way of a proper man. It was true that any man would be shocked to find their betrothed in this way, might even call off the marriage. But they wouldn't touch the woman, wouldn't hurt her. A sudden surprised grab perhaps, but they would have let go. Not Rodolfo.

"*Ahhh*," The nobleman began with a nefarious grin and a wicked little laugh. "Where are we off to this night, *mistress*?"

Noemi pulled against his hold on her arm. Though she could have tried a kindly voice to ease his grip, she was already angry. "Let go of me, *sir*. I go where I will. It is not your concern."

He continued to hold her tightly. Smiling, he pulled her up close. With a sour breath from drinking too many hours, he reminded her of their betrothal. "Oh, but it *izzzzz* my concern. You are *mine* now. Your mother and my father agree that we will marry. I was told today."

"As was I Rodolfo, but I tell you now that I do not consent and will not marry you. Forget such a match. I could not make you happy, nor would you make me so." She rebuked. "Now, let go of me!"

And yet, he held on. "Oh, but you *will* make me very, *very* happy. Shall I show you how? Isn't this what you were out seeking alone in the night? Doesn't the right belong to *me*?"

Her furry instantly turned to fear. He was threatening to force her right here in the alley. She slapped him hard across the face with her free hand

and pulled as forcefully away as she could. He let go, but only after he used his free hand to pull down the hood of her cloak, grabbing a fistful of her hair. He was far stronger than she was. As he took hold of her head, she was rendered helpless.

With no hope of getting away, she made to scream. She no longer cared who might hear. Her reputation was ruined regardless, already seen out alone at night by Rodolfo. He'd be sure to spread slanderous words about her slinking around the city in the dark; no one would believe that she was yet a maid. But as the shriek came up from her throat, Rodolfo turned her body to face away from him and slammed her hard against a cold stone wall. Her head smarted terribly by the fist in her locks and the smack to her forehead and face were fierce. She had never before experienced such an abuse.

Noemi began to feel dizzy as tiny white sparks danced before her eyes, her brain's reaction to the blow. She wondered whether this man would have assaulted her in this way if he had been sober at this moment, and instantly believed that he probably would. His future bride sneaking around the streets had allowed him to think of her as inferiorly as he'd wanted. And even if he had not discovered her and

they had married, he'd eventually have found some
displeasure with her to give him reason to do just what
he was doing now. A brute was a brute. Noemi was
terrified that she would collapse from the impact to her
head. Then he'd have a silent victim to mount, and she
would be a maid no more. She couldn't allow herself to
succumb; she had to fight.

In the moment that she dizzied, Rodolfo had
moved his hand from her hair to reach around the
front of her throat and had gripped her their around
her neck. Pushing her face up against the wall, she
could feel him pulling up the back of her cloak,
working to get up under her skirt. His grip was so tight
that she knew he could easily strangle her in his
violence. It was such that she could not scream out and
began to have trouble breathing. *How* would she fight?
Hadn't anyone heard this desperate interlude? Spied
them from their window? Though it was night,
someone *must* pass through. Or, was the fear of plague
keeping every Venetian so shut in?

And just then, as her face pressed against the wall
and Rodolfo tugged at her clothing, she saw a child in
the shadows just beyond. It was a pale little boy in only
a dirtied white chemise and dark pantaloons, his feet
bare and no winter covering to keep him warm. Had he

174

woke from the noises and hurried down from one of the apartments just above? Her eyes bulging with the strain, she watched how in an instant the boy was just beside them, as if his feet had not moved at all.

Why was he endangering himself? Why wasn't he running for help? She stared helplessly at the boy as even simple breaths became impossible. The monster's hold over her seemed far stronger than that of a mere man. It was the passion of his evil intentions that made him so ferine. Hadn't he seen the child? How could he go on?

But as her eyes met the boy's, a new horror crept into her. She recognized him for the very child that she'd just seen, dead in the back of the wagon that had passed by in the *calle*. It was he. The face was the very same, appearing more pallid than before. This was no flesh. He was a spirit.

Didn't you mean to survive on those pocketed gems? The boy asked. There was no movement to his lips, but only a voice she heard in her head. With his words, she remembered all that she had stuffed into her pockets. Quickly a shaking hand shot down and began rifling.

The precious items had all rattled loose of the fabric in which she had wrapped them and she could feel metal tangled and freely dispersed in the large pocket. And there, easily found by its shape, was her bejeweled crucifix. It had been crafted not to adorn her neck, but to hang on a chain from her waist. It was large at almost four inches long, and worked into sharp points at each arm, inlaid with dozens of dark garnets. Gripping it, she used her other hand to feel up and around behind her for Rodolfo's head, which was pressed against the back of her own. Using her touch and mind's eye to choose the spot, she stabbed him awkwardly but forcibly in the neck. The cross stuck in place, hardly to be believed. Rodolfo continued to rustle in her clothing for another few seconds before his grip loosened from her neck and his weight lifted slightly from her body. She used the precious moment to push back on him with all she had left, escaping from her trapped place.

Fire was in her eyes as she darted away, sucking in air, soon to stop, turn and stare at her attacker. There was no one else with them; the apparition of the boy was gone. Rodolfo looked aghast as he grappled the side of his neck. Blood was draining copiously around the glinting cross, where it was fearfully lodged. Rodolfo struggled to pull it out and did, only for the blood to flow more abundantly. The man was doomed, but Noemi could feel no sorrow. Anger and terror had entwined to create a deep hate within her breast. As she regained her breath, with a piteously damaged voice she uttered bitter words for her assailant.

"I yet a maid, and you now dead!" She looked possessed. Hair disheveled, clothes askew and eyes large and glossy with scorn. "You did not succeed in your crime against me, but you will pay for it now all the same..."

Panic-stricken, Rodolfo dropped the crucifix on the ground and then plunked down into a seated position with his hands, drenched in blood, clutching at his neck. The plush fabric of his noble dress saturated the flow. And though blood also covered Noemi's hands, she felt no mar upon her soul.

She flew over to his side like a witch, making the man wince. His voice remained caught in his throat by shock alone, as the injury had only damaged an unfortunate vein. But she had no intention of touching him again, only squatting down to retrieve her makeshift dagger. The formidable piece in her possession once more, she stood up and bolted away down the lane, quickly disappearing at a turn. Rodolfo fell back, knowing that he was soon to expire, unable to tell anyone the identity of his killer. Not a single Venetian was in the street this night to be at his dying side.

But wait...was that a boy? The ghoulish face hovered over him, looking curious. It was the last thing Rodolfo saw before Venice faded out and into darkness.

Fina

Aurelia and Fina felt very differently on the matter. The servants had fled several days before, but they were both resilient and intelligent young women who could do very well without a single one of them. The plague was now rife throughout the city and people were dying, sometimes out in the *calli*. Looking out of the second floor windows with their good views of the neighborhood, Fina had seen hardly a person passing through the local *campo* in the last days. She'd been disturbed one afternoon however to spot a destitute taken with the illness. At first, she thought he was dead; the helpless man was lying on the ground motionless. But then looking out the window again a half an hour later, she spied the body pulling itself over the stones for a few yards before it went still once more. The thought of even just one man dying alone in one of the city's squares was too much to bear. But what could she do? She prayed for God's forgiveness for not going out to help her fellow Venetian. At dusk, a passing corpse bearer collected the body.

Some did run through the labyrinth of streets like rushing ants on a mission toward deliverance, covering their faces with rags so as not to inhale the disease and often carrying bundles of goods. Where did they think they could go to escape, she had wondered. As Fina came to discover, Aurelia believed that though there was no way to fully escape, there at least might be a better place to reside.

Frosino hadn't risked the pestilence by walking out from his dwelling to theirs, but had sent a servant scurrying on his behalf. When the frenzied banging came to the door, Fina warned Aurelia that it might be imprudent to open it for anyone that they did not know. After communicating through the thick wood however, the lady of the house quickly acquiesced when she learned of the nature of the visit. Frosino, who'd grown very rich by trading in silk, maintained luxurious accommodations just a short distance away. He had been Aurelia's first patron in her role as a courtesan and though they'd dissolved their contractual agreement during the previous summer, it had been an amicable parting. At that time, Frosino was having desires for another courtesan and wanted to move on to her bed. This was *normale*; Venetian men of great income could exchange lovers as often as they liked.

Aurelia had lately heard that that courtesan had had the recent misfortune of growing out of favor with the Venetian government and had been exiled from the city. Courtesans often entertained great men with political ties and needed to dance artfully when speaking on matters concerning the republic. Clearly Frosino's consort hadn't been so careful with her words.

When he'd heard word of the threat of plague some months before, Frosino took careful measures to stock his *palazzo* well, thinking of every conceivable need. He was a smart man. And now that it was upon the city, he like everyone else was burrowing in and had even asked a party of friends to join him. More eccentrically than inviting guests during the world's apparent end, his lusty appetite didn't like the thought of celibacy until better times, and he didn't have a taste for any of the female servants he currently retained. Therefore, Aurelia was invited to rekindle their relationship until the emergency shared by all Venetians was at a place where travel was deemed safe, usually only a matter of a few months for most cities. She'd be well looked after, and compensated of course. She could even bring a maidservant, or a friend if it would please her.

Aurelia was immediately keen on the idea. Fina however, feared that the solicitation was only a glittering temptation in a dire situation. Leaving their fortress could end disastrously. After all, all of their servants had already fled; a sign that fear, death and chaos would ultimately rise within the city. Fina felt that since they were both in good health and could make do with the stores they had in the larder, that they should wait things out just where they were. All it would take was for just one of Frosino's servants to catch ill and spread it to them all. For instance, Frosino had allowed *this* attendant to act as messenger and pass through the *calli* to their house. What if the servant had stopped to ask after family? Frosino would continue to allow such mistakes to happen in the future, which would endanger them all.

In the end, Aurelia had won the debate. Fina had had the mind to remain behind, but Aurelia had raised good points about their safety as two ladies in a *palazzo* all on their own. Whenever the plague came, Venice's dregs were loosed from the prisons to work as collectors of the dead, but committed hideous crimes as they did. And even many who were not previously criminals, a handful of weak-natured citizens, *became* lawless when seeing the opportunity, breaking into homes to loot them; what of them? It would be safer to submit themselves to Frosino's care. Aurelia sent the servant back with her acceptance of the proposal. He should expect herself and one companion the following morning.

As the day moved on, Aurelia acted cheered while they packed just what clothes they could carry on the streets without becoming targets of plunder. All precious gems and items of gold were hidden away in the *palazzo* as best as could be. They would simply have to accept the risk that someone may break in during their absence. But as Aurelia put it, if it were fate for that to happen, at least *they* would be away some place safe when it did. The next morning, they locked the doors and footed the *calli* in haste to Frosino's.

Mafalda

Zeta told Mafalda about Paola's departure the moment she entered her chamber on the morning following. Setting down a tray of food on a side table, she described what a brave young woman she believed her to be. If it had been Zeta, she imagined she'd have cried a great deal before leaving the *palazzo*. But not Paola; she'd shed no tears.

While at her tidying, the maid came closer to where she sat and Mafalda noticed an opal ring set in a gold band on the servant's finger. She recognized it for Paola's. Had she no shame? First Tonia and now Zeta, stealing her little sister's belongings? She walked over and snatched up her hand. Holding it tight, she stared into the woman's eyes.

"Why are you wearing my sister's ring?" She asked with an accusatory tone.

Zeta told Mafalda about the gifts Paola had made to her and the others, even of how Paola had entreated her to learn how to write so that she might be her friend and exchange missives. Mafalda promptly let go of her hand and warmly apologized, asking Zeta's forgiveness. It was just such a difficult time and she was so ill at ease.

First washing her hands in a fresh basin of water, Mafalda soon sat to her little table to break her morning fast. The food was good and she was thankful that with the growing turmoil just outside, she was still able to eat in warmth, peace and comfort. Who knew how long that would last? But as she remembered her blessings, her heart also ached for her little sister. Though hundreds of Venetian noble ladies were placed in convents, and though it was also to be her fate almost directly, it was all happening so cruelly. They had none of them been able to say goodbye to their father, who had always been good and generous. Of all the girls, he'd especially doted on Paola because she was the youngest. It had always been evident how happy the littlest was, whenever their father joined the family for meals and entertainments. She sometimes even clung to him. Most noble fathers would have pushed their offspring away and called to their child's nursemaid, but he'd never chided her. He was always patient, smiled for her, kissed her forehead and amused her with harrowing tales from his travels on *terra firma*. Mafalda could cry even now, remembering how he'd shown his fatherly care for each of them as his children.

They had not always received his time and

patience in the recent years, but he was a very busy man. The girls were also considered women now, and their mother had undoubtedly reminded him of it. He needed to consider whether his daughters, as commodities, could be married in advantageous ways, or if they should be placed in nunneries for their permanent safekeeping. This was the tradition in all great houses.

Mafalda did not believe it was fair or right. She pondered what it would be like to live in a world where all women had the choice to decide their own destinies. And though what was taking place was common, the way everything was so harshly unfolding within *their* home was devastating. There was no family brought altogether to send their daughters to the nuns with decorum and love, and with promises to always be their connections to the world, with letters and visits. That was how it *should* have been. Paola should have gone to her enclosure at least knowing that she was loved and that she would never be forgotten. Mafalda would be leaving home in the same way. At the very least, they would be in the same convent, and a support for one another.

Had Fina not chosen another life for herself, had not had the availability of her friend Aurelia's home, or if she had been recouped by their mother, then she would have been with them as well. But Mafalda did not wish it. She was glad for her sister. The courtesan life would not always prove easy or opulent, but at least she'd found a way to free herself from convention.

If only there was a way that she could be free as well. But there was no place to go and even if she did run away, she'd be quickly forced to beggary. A highborn noblewoman lost everything by taking risks. Making an escape, or running to a lover, often led to penury and prostitution. Many a woman had wandered off to nowhere, never to be seen again.

And this was further reason for grief; where was Noemi? Was she safe? Who was she with? It was incredible that she sometimes knew so little about her sisters. She'd thought that they were all so much closer, but now she saw how easy it was for them to hide secrets. Noemi hadn't left aimlessly to anywhere; she'd gone somewhere, to someone. She wouldn't just leave home without some assurance for her safety. She wasn't a fool. Mafalda was surprised however, that Noemi had in fact *left*. It must have taken an inordinate amount of courage. And Fina! How had it slipped Mafalda's notice that her sister was preparing for the life of a courtesan? She had become rather vain. Had certainly spent more time reading over erudite topics, which bored Mafalda to sit and discuss. Had also been paying particular attention to perfecting her dance steps. And yet, she'd had no idea of Fina's plans.

It seemed her whole world was filled with secrets. What had happened to her father? Surely someone must know. Mirella had made so many inquiries, yet they still hadn't discovered his final whereabouts. And what about her mother? There seemed to be secrets there too. Mafalda had never been able to get close to her, and sometimes thought that she was strange for a mother. Mirella had never been cruel, but there was always a distance, coolness. Couldn't she even offer love and solace to her children during these hard times? After the loss of their father, with the passing of sweet Martinella, with the shock of Tonia's deceit and suicide, after Paola's brush with death, with the plague and panic that was all around them in the streets, and with their ultimate and unpredictable destinies in marriage or in the nunnery. How was it that a mother could offer no tenderness? In just a matter of months, so many painful things had happened.

Mirella soon called for Zeta from out in the hall, not so much as stepping into the room to share any words with her daughter. The servant opened the shutters over the windows before going. The light of the new day flooded in and Mafalda moved to sit for a time looking out toward the blue sky, watching the occasional pigeon flying past. Frost edged the windows and she was suddenly sad to realize that none of them would spend the winter festivities in Treviso as they always did. What a beautiful month it had been for them, just one year before. They'd all been so happy and healthy: Noemi glowed, Fina laughed, Paola danced, and even their mother had smiled and often. Orso had surprised them all by spending an entire week at the country villa, showering them with pretty gifts and thundering merrily around the house with his favorite hunting dogs lopping at his side. Those creatures stayed on *terra firma*. How fun it was to play with them as they went jumping and barking. She wondered what would happen to her father's dogs. Wondered whether their mother would even keep the estate.

Mafalda placed more wood on the fire and then bathed out of her basin, soon dressing in a simple modest dress. Perhaps it would be today, perhaps tomorrow, but soon she'd join Paola. There was no use coveting any precious possessions and fine gowns, as they could have no place with her. Perhaps she could lure Zeta with a kind reward, if she would but sell her gems for her after the plague subsided. Zeta could use the money to bring Paola and Mafalda special treats and little treasures on feast days, and during the *Carnevale*. She'd already befriended Paola, perhaps she could be a friend to them both. Mafalda, as with all of her sisters, had acquired many special adornments made of jewels and gold. The money from them could help supplement some of Paola and Mafalda's needs if their mother didn't continue to provide for them once they were gone from her sight. What if they needed some yards of cloth or a block of soap? Despite being in the care of the nunnery, and their noble parents arranging a yearly contribution to the establishment on their behalf, it was still the responsibility of a woman's family to procure enough income for their daily needs, like clothing and linens. Perhaps Zeta might even sneak them books and other forbidden items for their amusement!

For a time, she gathered such items as would be found valuable; she would indeed entreat Zeta to help them, and hope that she could trust her to follow through. She would hand every last ornament to her, except for one. Mafalda had had the large pearl that Baldovino gave her set into gold prongs. It now hung on a gold chain. As all Venetian women did, she loved pearls. Venice was tied to the sea and their very life was surrounded by it. Their tables were covered by the fruit of the waters and premiered precious silver boxes of sea salt. Women went covered in pearls, while merchants gained great wealth by mastering ships. Their very homes were built into the waters and they traveled by boat through winding canals far more than they walked. She would keep this one necklace. She put it over her head and tucked it safely under the white cotton of her shift.

As she did so, she heard a horrible wailing from outside, and it made her heart take pause. Here she was only thinking of herself, of the goods that Zeta could smuggle for her and her sister, when people were taking ill in their houses. Mafalda had never seen anyone sick with the plague, only those sketched illustrations in books and one particularly fearsome painting displayed in their church. That canvas had been there since before she'd been born. It had scared her out of her wits as a little girl. She'd prayed hard that the scary skeletons in the painting, Death's army roaming in search of plague victims, would never come to Venice for her family.

She closed her eyes now and prayed once more,

something she'd been remiss in doing for quite some time. There were people suffering, her very neighbors. She prayed that the House of Orso would be spared, as well as the convent she was soon to enter. How could Mirella have allowed Paola to go yesterday, with the disease encroaching all around them? How would she now insist that Mafalda go too? Couldn't she have kept them both safe at home and waited for the danger to abate?

There simply was no understanding such persistence. Mirella clearly wanted her affairs settled after the death of her husband, plague or no. Mafalda wondered if it wasn't something to do with grief. Perhaps her mother was grieving her husband and couldn't stand the sight of her own daughters, the very fruit of their marriage. That could be the reason for her mother's hurry to get her children settled so soon after Orso had fallen eternally silent. Grief was a strange thing.

The door to her room creaked open once more and Mafalda opened her eyes as Zeta came in. Perhaps she'd come back to clear away her breakfast, or perhaps it was the very hour that she was to meet her fate. Was it time to leave home?

"Mistress, I would not have dared to break your

mother's rules if I were one of your permanent servants. But I am not, and not beholden to her will. Your mother, she is in the kitchen taking an inventory of the stores. I snatched the keys from her bedchamber and am quickly come to say that the plague has afflicted several nuns at your sister's convent. As you well know, it is often months before new converts take their initial vows, so your sister wouldn't be committing any sin to leave it, even if only temporarily for her safety. But, your mother will not go to retrieve her for fear that the pestilence might be spread through her." Zeta shook her head mournfully.

"I told her the news myself, for my brother delivers firewood there three times a week by boat, which he does also for my house, your neighbor, the House of Iacopo. I have just seen him at the canal. He was at the convent at sunrise. The guardian nun from behind the door instructed through the grate that he *leave* the wood just before the entrance, rather than bring it *into* the foyer of the convent where he is usually trusted to drop it. When he asked why so, he was warned that there were some fallen sick within." Zeta blurted the last frightful words with the quickness of morning birds in their chatter.

"Oh Zeta, no!" Mafalda gasped.

"It is the truth. I am so sorry to deliver this news and will be saying my prayers for Paola. I plan to leave this house soon, Mafalda. Your mother looks to be readying to board up the *palazzo* and my brother wishes me to go with him to our mother's in Murano. It will be no more secure than here I suppose, but I will feel safer with my family. If we're chosen for death, at least we'll be together." She further shared.

With a sad smile, Zeta moved nearer and squeezed Mafalda's hand. It was oddly clammy, surely from the servant's frenzied rush to deliver the news. There was no use now asking her to sell her treasures, what a childish plan. Mafalda couldn't be sent to the convent now. Paola would be alone. Would their little sister survive?

Even though she understood her mother's fears, she couldn't believe that Mirella wouldn't risk retrieving her own child before it was too late. The nuns would have enough on their hands and would be thankful to have one less ward to look after, especially seeing as Paola was so new to their residence. With any luck, Paola would have remained private as she spent her first night and day in her new cell, getting her bearings and arranging her trunks. If so, it would be unlikely that she'd been exposed. Their mother still had time!

"I am not certain when we are to leave, my brother will come for me. It could be as soon as tomorrow night. I must return your mother's keys now, and quickly. But lo, I discovered another set amongst your father's letters when Mirella bid me sweep his chamber yesterday. I will go and seek them out and get them to you before I away. At least then, you will not be a prisoner." Zeta nodded reassuringly and then retreated in haste, locking the door behind her.

Though the serving woman could have set her free just then, it had been wise to wait. Zeta needed to get out of the house and away from Mirella *before* it was discovered that she had enabled another daughter's escape. Further, Mafalda didn't have a plan. If she had run out of the door with Zeta just now, where would she have gone? The nuns wouldn't hand Paola over to her without their mother's permission. And even if they did, where would they have fled after that? Mafalda had to think.

Mirella

The world was falling apart. She'd taken account of the supplies they had and felt that it was enough to see Mafalda, a handful of servants and herself through for a few months if necessary. Her second born wouldn't be going to the nunnery so soon. Even without the news about what had befallen the convent, Mirella had felt uneasy about taking another boat outing through the canals. The city had become eerie and the plague was spreading; one never knew what they might encounter. She would not be moved to take any more risks for fear of the contagion. She'd shut up the House of Orso, and they would wait.

There were six servants in the dwelling, including one that was temporary. She'd send Zeta back and only retain the last five, four women and one man. Leaving the kitchen to rest in her room, she encountered Meo heading to her chamber with a bundle of firewood in his arms. It had become increasingly frigid outside and the fires needed continual tending. Mirella instructed Meo to use the wood sparingly. Until further notice, only her room, Mafalda's room, the servants' quarters and the kitchen were to remain heated. They needed to reserve all they had.

Upon hearing her instruction, confusion showed on his face. "Will Mafalda be coming back from the convent, m'lady?"

"Whatever do you mean, Meo?" Mirella asked curtly.

"I saw her at the waterside, not a quarter hour past. She wears a blue velvet cloak, no? I thought she was taking her place beside Paola at the convent today. As I didn't see your ladyship, I guessed that Zeta or Penina were about, ready to accompany her." Meo explained bashfully. He could sense that something was amiss by the look on Mirella's face. He shifted uncomfortably, the pile of wood becoming heavier with each passing second.

Feigning fatigue, she placed her hand up to her forehead and nodded confirmation of what he was telling her. "Yes, yes Meo. Do you believe my children are all gone from me? It is hard on a mother."

The servant looked relieved, nothing was wrong but that the lady was tired. Of course it was difficult for her. What with her husband gone, Fina rumored to be a courtesan, Noemi missing and two other daughters gone to the convent. No one yet knew where Noemi was. What unexpected rebelliousness! However, it was easy to understand why Mirella could not make a greater attempt to search her out. The city had gone cold and quiet. And though Orso's men, those trusted fellows now employed to Mirella until all of her affairs were settled, those men who would usually have sought out a missing daughter for their mistress, they were now locked up in their own houses waiting out the pestilence.

Meo offered his lady a consoling nod and then moved on to fill the woodpile in her bedchamber, soon leaving her alone. Mirella contained her surprise at Mafalda's passage out of the *palazzo*, in spite of feeling completely stupefied by what Meo had told her. She didn't even make the effort to go to her daughter's room to confirm it. So Mafalda had fled too! What good would it do to try and chase her? She had no men able to seek her out and drag her back. Only Mirella and Zeta had known of the plague in the convent; if Meo had known of it as well, he would have been puzzled at why she was going there. He would have stopped to speak to her himself. But he had not known, and Mafalda had disappeared in daylight.

Who let her free? She could only assume it was Zeta. Before the plague, Mirella would have punished a servant severely for such a misdeed. But now that Mafalda had made her choice, she would wipe her hands of them all. Zeta certainly wouldn't receive the pay she was owed, and Mafalda would not be allowed back into the house. Not after sneaking away, and especially not after potentially exposing herself to disease in the *calli*. Her daughter had doomed herself with just one step outside of her safe haven. Zeta had certainly informed Mafalda of the sickness pervading the nunnery, as well as Mirella's refusal to go back for Paola. Perhaps that was where Mafalda had gone, fleeing to save her sister. What a fool.

Paola. The child's words struck her once more. The sweets that Mirella had passed on, the very ones intended for *her* from her husband. Had those confections truly been the source of the poison in the house? But there had also been a nightshade berry found and named by Martinella; hadn't it been Tonia's? Sitting before the fire, she worked the puzzle over in her thoughts. She'd received a lap-sized chest of gifts from Orso, just as she usually did when he was away for extended periods. Sometimes they contained supple leather gloves, or scented handkerchiefs or beautiful writing paper. The offerings tended to be simple, yet thoughtful. Mirella's heart felt unexpectedly moved to think of it; those small gifts of affection from husband to wife.

She'd received the chest not very long after Orso
had been thought missing, which would mean that
he'd sent it around the time he'd last been seen.
Mirella didn't know who had delivered the chest. Orso
had commissioned any number of runners over the
years to transfer letters, goods and gifts back to *Venezia*.
If it were a familiar man, Meo always recognized them
when they entered the house, and left their pay to
Orso, who settled accounts in his time. But for smaller
deliveries, when Orso made a quick hire from off some
village street to travel back to Venice, Meo would pay
them a rightful sum of coins from a coffer that he'd
been placed in charge of.

A frightening question entered her mind. What if
the chest had been sent *after* Orso should have been
considered dead? What if he'd never met with his end
at all, and had indeed sent sugary poisons to end his
wife's life from wherever he resided? Was her husband
alive? It had been many months, with no sign of him at
all. She immediately thought to question Meo. Perhaps
he could remember who had delivered the gifts. Was it
someone he'd met before? Perhaps he'd had some
conversation with the man? The individual might have
mentioned *something*, such as when the delivery had
been arranged with Orso, and in which town they'd

transacted.

As Mirella descended a marble stair away from her chamber and toward the first floor, she could hear a terrible howl from without the residence. By the way the sound carried, it was surely a man in agonies floating down the canal by boat. Was he being transported to a doctor, or worse, to one of the terrible quarantine islands? Mirella paused, wondering if it wasn't useless to pursue Meo. After all, even if Orso had survived and plotted against her, what were the chances that he was well and living right now? The plague had swept through the countryside *first*, and he'd certainly have encountered it by boarding in an inn, or securing any needs with local townspeople.

It was a far worse death than the one *she'd* conspired for him. This pained her; she'd meant to end of him, but not for him to suffer. If he'd died of the plague, he had suffered. As she continued slowly down the stairs, the cries from the water faded away and she regained her motivation to carry on. After not finding Meo in any of the anticipated places, she headed toward the kitchen once more. The rooms along the way were growing dim and drafty, their fires working towards their ends after Mirella's direction to save on wood. Upon finding the kitchen empty, she began to grow agitated. Clearly her servants were lazing in their rooms, as no one was anywhere to be seen. However, when she went to look, she didn't find them there either, and their small, individual room fires were going out; they hadn't been kept going. Where *were* they? But to ask the question was foolish. She already knew that the servants, unless she came upon one yet, had without any notice left the House of Orso.

It was not entirely surprising. Once they'd caught on that Mirella was counting stores and limiting firewood, and with listening to those cries just outside the doors, they'd became restless and decided amongst themselves to hurry off to the homes of loved ones rather than stay here to serve her. Though noblewomen weren't meant to make their own meals, feed their own fires or empty their own chamber pots, she was a dexterous woman and cared little that they'd gone. To hell with everyone who'd disobeyed her, fled her, abandoned her and defied her! She'd lock up every entrance; she'd survive it all while Venice heaved. Eventually out of her hibernation, she'd live on to be one of the wealthiest nobles left to the city.

But as she began to make her rounds to ensure that every door was bolted and that the ground floor windows were secure, there came a crashing sound from one of the rooms above. It sounded to be about the place where Mafalda's bedchamber was, or perhaps even, it was her own. Had someone climbed up to a second floor window and gained access into her house? Or was one of the servants still within the dwelling after all? There was only one way to find out.

Fina

Even though she had lived on this island for all of her life, and had so rarely set foot on *terra firma*, Fina felt that it must be rare to find a city so markedly unique. No place was such a conundrum, such a strange mirage, as was Venice. Here, one could be anyone they wished, transcending reality, even with just the simple change of a mask.

As they sat to Frosino's decadent table, she watched Aurelia mesmerize the man with impressive ease. When had her friend come to develop such a wit, such a sharp intelligence and such a charming manner? Fina could hardly recognize her as the playmate of her youth, that simple sweet friend with plain looks. The girl she had so often confided in and known so well. Aurelia wasn't Aurelia anymore.

Frosino laughed boisterously as his courtesan presented him with posed faces and gestures. Aurelia was making him guess the great Venetian men she was mimicking. The woman had become an actress, a convincing one at that. Frosino, though glittering with riches and fine clothes, had no particular delicacy. In a way, he reminded Fina of her father. He banged a fist upon the table repeatedly, an act of pleasure for

Aurelia's performance. At that moment, he knocked over an empty goblet, the loud clanking and sight of which made Fina startle and then softly laugh. A servant girl quickly scurried in to set the cup aright and fill it.

Some several other couples were sprinkled along the table. The stage was extravagant, like something out of a garish dream. Though the feast was just as fine as any ever given in the House of Orso, the scene was acutely more colorful and jarring. And amidst these courtesans and their lovers, the men were showing little restraint while every woman behaved sensually, excepting Fina. The language that drifted past her ears was base, filled with political critique that would not have been safe to whisper among larger circles. Everyone said what he or she thought without care. The salacious conversation too, was new to her.

Here, a pair of wine-stained lips met. There, a man caressed a breast just under the bodice line without even the woman making a modest gasp. And there, another woman's hand wandered beneath the table to squeeze her lover's thigh. Everywhere, good wine flowed while fleshy oysters slid down spoiled throats. There was the tinkling of priceless engraved glass amidst the murmuring, with the crackling of an enormous fire to provide the music. There was an artful restraint among the couples as they played, each enjoying the general seduction until moving to their individual chambers. But even with the perversity of the guests, Fina couldn't help but find the display stunning. It was hard to believe that she was one of the characters in this play.

All before her *was* a play. For what else could it be when one considered the threat looming from without the doors? Acting was the *only* way each guest assembled could keep up with such a show while Venetians perished just outside, some of them their own kin. Fina shuddered and thought of her sisters. Why wasn't the tone dimmed, the twinkle less? *Only* in Venice. Each of them might be as anxious as she, yet were using this moment as a defying interlude, spitting in the eye of Death. Tonight, they were eluding the plague and living loudly. She wondered what would happen if just one amongst the party began to perspire unreasonably, or began to cough persistently. Would they screech and scatter? Or would they laugh more loudly than before, caress more brazenly and ignore the truth until they themselves succumbed to the plague just where they sat?

Mondin gently touched her hand, stirring her

from her thoughts, reminding her that she in fact *did* have a role to play tonight. She shifted slightly to face him where he sat beside her. Mondin was handsome, tall with a muscular frame. She carefully slid her hand away to rest on her lap. Smiling, she felt herself instantly blush. His black hair was shorn close to his head, while shadowy whiskers cleanly trimmed covered his cheeks and chin. One of his ears was pierced, studded with a dark ruby. The nobleman's clothes were very fine. He wore a fitted doublet of glossy black damask patterned with gold thread. He smelled like spice, sweet oranges mixed with nutmeg. He was alluring.

As Fina had observed Mondin throughout the evening, she believed that even though he reacted with genuine pleasure to the mischievous behavior of his acquaintances, he had so far acted discreetly. In spite of much deep and full laughter and a beguiling smile to compliment the merry banter in the room, he'd spoke and behaved in no way offensively. He'd uttered no joke that was unkind or piercing, nor had he attempted any flirtation to skirt the crude. He spoke comfortably and intelligently. She thought that he could be a man she could like, and yet she had trouble moving in any direction to entertain him. All she could muster was to act her self all evening, making no real attempt to captivate him. She provided only plain conversation broken up by long bouts of silence. How could she have ever believed she could be a courtesan?

"You have a lovely smile, *bella* Fina." He said with convincing warmth.

Mondin's green eyes, framed by dark lashes, were entrancing. Fina couldn't look away and imagined that her cheeks were blushing crimson. This was ridiculous. *She* was supposed to be inventing compliments to win *him*, not the other way around.

"Thank you, Lord Mondin." Fina returned, her voice grainy. She nervously cleared her throat and offered him another smile. Mondin chuckled.

"Is that all? You will not favor me in return? And I believed *every* courtesan was a fountain of nectarous words!" Mondin's remark was tickling and his smile smooth.

Fina laughed lightly and shook her head. She grabbed for her white satin fan and began to sway it back and forth before her face, strands of her dyed blond hair gently moving in the breeze.

"*Mmm*, yes. Courtesans *are* expected to laud their guests. But as I am sure you already know sir...I have never received a man before. I am unpracticed." She confided.

"*Received* a man?" Lord Mondin baited.

His question embarrassed her. He was gently teasing her for being yet a maiden. She couldn't escape the obviousness of her innocence, so clearly marked on her face and stamped across her breast, which nervously rose and fell with each breath above her silk bodice. She cleared her throat once more.

"Received...*entertained* a man. At a banquet such as this, Lord Mondin." Fina suddenly had the urge to get up and walk away from the feast table. She felt immature, unprepared. "I assure you, I will be slow to say or do the expected thing. Perhaps you have chosen the wrong companion to dine beside you this night."

"Why do you say this, fair Fina? Because your blush is pure and not paint, as is Aurelia's tonight? Because your eyes are not lustrous and round by drops of nightshade as are Zuana's? Or is it because you cannot entice a man with a snake's tongue, with cunning and gossip, like Mari?" Mondin laughed, reached for his goblet and drank. He expectantly watched for Fina's reaction over the rim.

Fina glanced around the room at the other courtesans, inspecting Mondin's observations. She shook her head and sighed, paused her fanning and took a sip from her chalice. The gold drops hanging from her ears reflected the firelight while the heady red liquid colored her lips.

"But are not those exactly the qualities which make a courtesan so captivating? Isn't *that* what you were seeking tonight by chancing the canals to eat at Frosino's table? Did you not come to be bewitched?" She paused for another sip from her goblet, set down the vessel, and then returned the man's gaze. "Let us not play a charade, Lord Mondin. You came to be pleasured in public. In private too, by a woman such as *these*." Fina was surprised by her own directness as she swept her fan out over the table.

She knew that she should have tried harder. Tried to be whimsical, interesting, and provocative. But in her heart, she wasn't able to forget the farce that was this night. Fina had abandoned her precious sisters to gain her freedom. And though she had indeed escaped her mother's grip, she was yet a captive. The reality of this was painfully beginning to sink in with jagged edges. She had entered a lifetime of pleasing patrons for survival. Just as terrible, the threat of death hovered just outside. Creeping past the windows, tapping at the doors, laughing from the shadows. It might even have made its way in with Mondin.

She shivered as he gently brought his hand up to her cheek, but she didn't push it away. He caressed it, and then drew his fingers along the hairline above her ear. She placed her fan down on the table, defeated by the tenderness detected in Mondin's touch. She stared into his eyes, the movement and babble around them fading away with the words that followed.

"I can see your dark hair here, where no dye has reached. It is a beautiful color." When he retracted his hand, she wanted it back. "You are mistaken mistress. I am not seeking a courtesan. I am searching for something else entirely. A lover yes, but only one who will also agree to be my wife."

Mafalda

As Mafalda's lashes flickered open to only the dimness of a fading firelight, she lethargically watched as shadows moved along the empty stone wall that was the view before the bed. For a moment, she once again could not remember where she was or how she had gotten there, but the pains in her body quickly helped remind her. In spite of the aching, she at least felt safe in the warmth and quiet of the room. She considered the wall that stretched out before her and how bare it was. Fina would need to hang a tapestry to cover those stones and bring some cheer to the room; a garden scene filled with lush trees, blossoming flowers, and bounding creatures. Her eyes moved up to the top of the thick bedposts and to the formidable beams lining the lofty ceiling. The long bolster beneath her head felt blessedly soft, while a crumpled coverlet that partially covered her body was smooth and comforting.

Though it was a strain to do so, her muscles stiff and sharp pains striking in many places to cause her to wince, she perched up upon her elbows to take in the rest of the room. She wished that she could bathe in a full tub of steamy water and sip one of Martinella's soothing broths. These things would have gone a long way to help her regain some strength, but at least for now she'd had some sleep before a fire. She could never have understood the magnificence of such simple conveniences before now.

As there was no one there to help her, she would have to fight the urge to lie back down and go to sleep again so soon. She needed to eat something, and it would also be prudent to more fully clean the broken sores that would now be asking to heal. She would take her time. She would place more wood on the fire and build it up again. She would wrap herself warmly with the fur blanket bunched up next to her and shuffle back down those cold stairs to the kitchen, perhaps even manage to heat a kettle of water. But as she went perched, her head as heavy as stone and urging her to lie back down, her hair matted and malodorous around her face, she glimpsed one of her pale, uncovered feet.

Mafalda gasped and whimpered. What more? She had already been through so much! She had survived the pestilence, had crawled from her grave, had mortally stabbed a man, and had nearly drifted out to sea in a dark, frozen slumber. She'd suffered through illusions of the dead speaking to her, the woman's corpse with the blackened eye. Mafalda must have unconsciously spied the blade herself, the only thing that she could use to protect herself from the *beccamorto* out of the heap where she lay. But in her skewed imagination, the dead woman had startled her into taking action to save herself.

She had also faced Baldovino, whom she loved, during her most desperate hour. Only, he had already been dead for days, and his father too. These speaking specters had been her imagination. They'd died from the plague, had only appeared to her at the height of her desolation. The memory of it at just this moment scared her into believing she would go mad, or more likely already was. She searched her hands, bruised and ugly from breaking the lock on the *palazzo* door herself. No other living human had been there to see her scurry around the building and break entry to get in. Baldovino and Santino had only been friendly figures in the shadows of her mind as she searched for warmth and shelter. Or, perhaps they *had* been ghosts.

Might another appear now? Another spirit to help her do what must be done? A slow, piercing call moved out from her lips as her eyes squinted with dread and fresh tears. Two of her toes on her right foot were completely dead and black, their rot nearly reaching the still living meat of her foot. Too long had those tender feet gone frozen in the pit, and now toes would be lost for it. Further, she wouldn't live if she didn't hurry to cut them off. She hoped that they hadn't already poisoned her veins. Prayed that she wouldn't lose too much blood in the cutting of them. She needed to be quick in seeking out a sharp and heavy knife.

After the horrible task was done, under unbearable minutes of panic and pain, Mafalda lay panting over the comfortless stones of the kitchen floor while ample tears made her blind. Sleek and sticky with blood, a blade was clutched in her hand once more. This time two toes, stiff and morbid, were her victims. She sobbed, squeezing her eyes shut hard. The echoes of her own travailing made her remember another desperate moment, just some few days in the past.

In her mind, she could see once more, Zeta dropping the ring of iron keys as she collapsed. How they'd clattered on the stone. Mafalda had scrambled toward her from the window where she'd been deeply mourning the news, anxiously fondling the pearl hanging from her neck and praying for her future. The serving woman, so young and healthy, began to moan. Mafalda could immediately see that Zeta's neck showed an unnaturally red and swollen round near her collarbone. Her face was glossy with dampness and her eyes were round and fitful.

How fast it had happened. Just that day Zeta had promised to steal Orso's keys for her. But before a half an hour had passed, she'd returned unexpectedly, still dangerously carrying the set she'd filched from Mirella. Zeta had crossed paths with the servant Penina who had heard disturbing news while in conversation with a passing tradesman through a grated window. Poor Santino and his family! Zeta had quickly run back to tell Mafalda what she had learned, had clasped her in her arms when Mafalda had made a silent scream into her fists. Had hugged and swayed her for a moment, but was soon pressed to hurry out again. She was going to get Mafalda those keys *now*, and then leave the *palazzo* herself. The plague surrounded them. She would seek out her brother and they would go home.

As she kneeled close beside her, too afraid to touch her, Mafalda frantically called out her name. She wanted to shake her, to somehow startle her out of danger even though she knew that she was powerless. Zeta had been so kind to her while she'd been locked in her chamber, had risked stealing Orso's keys for her, even in her last healthy hour. More, she'd understood her secret. Had learned of her nights with Baldovino.

All of the household servants, though discreet, had known. No noble in Venice could keep secrets from their servants; they were the very stones of the *palazzi*, with eyes in every corner.

After a quick succession of coughs and then an intake of raspy breath, Zeta's face turned toward the door of the chamber. She feebly lifted an arm and pointed toward it. Zeta was not only brave; she was a saint. Regardless of her own discomfort and fear, she was pointing out an opportunity for Mafalda to breakout. And Zeta was right. The plague had found its way into the House of Orso. Mafalda should not tarry another second, or it would be certain death. She would go immediately to Paola, would extricate her, would find a way. After that, well she just didn't know.

"Hurry, *sorella*." Zeta sputtered.

Sister, she had called her, followed with more coughing. The servant then turned into herself, into the floor, as if in much pain.

Quickly standing, Mafalda was nearly as much terrified for herself as she was for Zeta. The House of Orso was crumbling and the walls of Venice were creaking inward with their heaviness, ready to fall. She turned away, hurried from Zeta toward the open door, and ran toward life. She slipped through with a soft swish of her gown and skirted the walls along the hall with caution. She carried no gold and no jewels, save the pearl that hung at her neck. Quietly she went, her heart beating fast at the chance of being caught. A shadow of shame hung over her for having abandoned Zeta, even though she knew she had to. At the same time, Baldovino's name repeated itself again and again. She could have collapsed and sobbed for it, but mourning this black day would have to wait. She slinked past the stones of her youth, moved through the place like a determined thief. She fled down marble steps like a startled cat, soon finding herself just before the entry of the kitchen with its dockside portal.

Servants would see her running through. She hoped that they would move aside to let her pass, that not one would move to stop her. She prayed too, that they would remain mute to the fierce questioning that would come. She had to be bold; this was her way to freedom, and perhaps Paola's only hope for escape too. But as she moved to enter the kitchen, she ran straight into Penina, figure full and face red with work and hurry. She was a strong, hardworking woman to wash the sheets and scrub the chamber pots.

"Oi! What now? *Mafalda*? An' ye not in yer room

mistress? How now? Where do you go? Hath the lady let you about the house?" She huffed with confusion.

Penina looked more upset about the jostle than she did about her mistress's surprising movements through the *palazzo*. However, Mafalda could not hide her look of urgency and frenzied shifting. The servant would know.

"An' where do ye go girl, in such a hurry?" Penina asked as she tried catching her breath, a plump hand full over her heaving breast. The woman's cotton cap lay askew, crooked over her head.

Mafalda did not answer. She hesitated, uncertain whether she should scamper past or plea to Penina for help. The woman looked into her eyes and then suddenly squinted with understanding. It was as though she could read her thoughts.

"Ai, *no* mistress!" Penina frowned. The serving woman moved her hand away from her breast only to wring both of her hands in her greasy apron.

"I know why you're running. Gossip is fast, though not so quick as this plague! It be the son of Santino, aye?" She shook her head, sure of what she said. "Yes, he was a goodly youth, but ye can't outrun yer pain lady. There be *nowhere* to hide from it, the grief will find you. And otherwise, there be *no* safe place outside these walls, m'lady."

At that moment, Penina's eyes went from squinting to large rounds. She quickly clutched Mafalda's shoulders with some sudden thought. Glancing warily around herself, she then whispered the revelation. "Your menses mistress! When were they last?"

Penina had scrubbed every scrap of linen in the house since Mafalda had been an infant. There'd been no soiled rags, no sullied undergowns, nor even a stained bed covering to come from her chamber for some months. Could she be pregnant? Of course it could be so, though she'd yet to have the sickness that came in the morning for women growing with a child. There had been so much stress to distract her. No room in her thoughts to suspect what might be going on in her womb.

"Fall to your knees before your mother. She will know best for ye. That woman is clever enough to get ye married in a fortnight...though this scourge might get in the way. Oh, my heart." Penina would have embraced her if it weren't for the strange look in Mafalda's eyes. She had much sweat on her brow. Was it on account of her grief and surprise? Or was it more?

Mafalda felt it then. The mean twinge at the back

of her throat, the heat beneath her skin and the ache in her spine. She was not well. Of course she wasn't. Zeta had served her these past days. They were *both* sick. Penina could see it too, released her hold and moved away, making the sign of the cross over her body.

As she lay coiled now, her amputated toes strewn on the stones, blackened and stiff, she felt the extreme parch in her throat. She'd yet to drink anything but souring wine. She suddenly cried out for Martinella with a dry call. The servant had cared for her and her sisters more than Mirella ever had. Thus, she'd loved her like a mother. Tragic that the old woman could not come when she needed her the most, could not even hear her call from where she slumbered eternally.

She'd wanted to cry out for Martinella then too, that moment she'd slumped down before the servant, but she fainted instead. Penina had quickly yelled out for help. Another serving woman, Antea, came running down the hall at that exact moment, screaming for help herself. She had discovered Zeta. Mafalda couldn't remember how she'd been moved, only becoming conscious in Fina's room, lying between the sheets in her sister's vacant bed. Was she not in her own chamber because Zeta was being tended there? Did Zeta still live?

It was nearly impossible to stay alert. Mafalda could vaguely hear herself whimpering, the fever and aches causing her pain unlike anything she'd ever experienced. She fell in and out of consciousness, again and again while firelight and strange shadows crept around her. It was night. When waking one last time at what must soon be dawn, she sensed her end was near. She opened her eyes, but they were suspended. She could not command them to move.

Mafalda was overcome with dread, cold sweat encompassing her body to warn her that eternal silence was approaching. She could feel it coming; this was the dawn of her death. She asked God for deliverance while with silent eyes, she watched her mother come into view. Mirella approached the bed, reached out tenderly for one of her clammy hands and squeezed it gently. She quickly pulled it away however, commanding a servant to call for a *beccamorto*.

"But lo! *Mother*! I am not gone!" She screamed from unmoving lips.

Mafalda had cried inside, had beat her hands upon the bed in her mind, had shed tears that would go unseen as her mother trailed out of the room. She watched her form stop at the door and falter there, soon to stand erect and disappear out of sight. This was all that was ever to be remembered before waking in the pit.

Mirella

As she toed in haste back up marble stairs, she kept an ear open for the source of the clanging she had heard just minutes before. She quickly dismissed the idea that an intruder had broken into the *palazzo*. More likely, she'd been premature in believing that all her servants had fled. Just less than an hour ago she'd been speaking with Meo; he would be about his work somewhere. One of the servants would soon appear, for it could only have been one of them to make the noise. A dropped platter? A broken stool?

As she stepped up into the long shadowy hall, lined with chambers including her own, she suddenly felt just how large her house was. This was not the only such hall, for there was yet another floor above, just as there was below. The palace was a behemoth of stone. Night was coming and the place was growing dim, lacking the usual robust fires in each room while the candles went unlit. It had never felt so enormous to her before as it had always been bustling with servants, the girls, guests, and sometimes the boisterousness that was Orso's heavy feet, clashing sword belt, and thunderous voice.

Far down the hall to her right, she spied Mafalda's

224

door ajar with a snatch of warm light pouring out. She stopped to listen and watch, believing she heard muffled coughing in that direction. Was Meo putting out the fire in her daughter's newly abandoned chamber? She thought she spied a shadow moving past the doorway and readied to walk toward the room, but then heard a strange shuffle to her left in the direction of her own chamber. Never before a skittish woman, Mirella began to feel uneasy. She considered calling out, demanding anyone near to walk out into the hall, but she couldn't make herself do it. The house was feeling uncanny to her just then.

Quietly she moved toward her own doorway. Perhaps the noise had come from there. Was it Penina? Had Zeta foolishly remained in the house after releasing Mafalda from her room? Was it Antea come to sweep the stones? Just as she was about to pass into the large chamber, with its last bit of gloomy winter light seeping in from a high window and its rosy glow from the fire, she glimpsed an adumbral figure passing into her anteroom in the far corner. Mirella startled, stopped before the passage and began to feel her heart pick up pace in her chest.

She'd seen the person for but a mere second before they'd slipped into the small, drafty room where

Mirella safely kept her trunks of linens, precious chests and a tall wardrobe filled with furs and gowns. She couldn't even determine if it had been a man or a woman. The body had looked tall and draped. Covered by a cloak? She wanted to shout out, draw out all the hidden servants. She wanted to send Meo in to apprehend the intruder in her private closet while the ladies of her household stood nearby with her as witnesses. Who was in her chamber?

But to raise her voice was an unnecessary disturbance. She was the mistress of this house and had no reason to be afraid. She would confront the person within herself. Drawing in a fortifying breath, Mirella moved into her room while keeping her eyes on the open door of her stony closet. The only sounds were the rustle of her hem as it swept across the stones, and the popping of fiery embers. If any larger noise broke out at that moment, it would have caused her to screech in surprise. Inching along toward the door of that inner room, she finally stood before it and cautiously peered inside. Mirella imperceptibly jolted and let out a hushed gasp. Two white eyes were staring out at her! But wait, it was not the trespasser.

She'd viewed the portrait a thousand times before when it had hung on the walls in her chamber, but had forgotten that she'd arranged to have it moved into the anteroom. Orso, handsome and commanding from his large canvas, stood propped against a stony wall. The servants believed she'd wanted it dismounted and set away because she grieved each time she looked upon it. Only Mirella knew that it sparked more guilt than grief. But there with Orso, in the recesses of that dark room, stood the figure she was seeking. Cloaked and hooded, they too silently observed the painting while facing away from Mirella. The form appeared in reverie, perhaps not even sensing that Mirella was there.

The stranger's cloak had a deep blue color to the fabric and Mirella instantly wondered if it was not Mafalda! Had not Meo thought he'd seen her on the waterside in her blue cloak? Had she come back into the house? Had she wanted to take in one last look of her father's portrait? This was all too strange. But then a disturbing thought came to her. Perhaps Meo had not seen Mafalda outside at all. Perhaps this was someone *unknown*. Not someone escaping to leave, but someone who had made their way inside.

"Reveal yourself." Mirella managed to say with an authoritative tone.

As the figure turned around to face her, Mirella

was met with a familiar visage. It was her *sister*. Yet, so changed, aged and beaten, that she believed at once that Lagia must have risen from her plague grave to seek revenge upon her. The color drained from Mirella's face, overcome with fright. This could be no nightmare; she was fully awake! Was this a ghost? Was it an admonitory vision, or a terrifying spirit to threaten punishment for all her past sins? What should she do? Scream? Flee? But Mirella could do nothing, remaining frozen in place while she stared at the woman who for so many years had gone a stranger.

Mafalda

Every stolen moment with Baldovino was one she knew she shouldn't be having. It had all begun the very moment the pearl was in her hand. Constant thoughts of him began to pervade her mind. His eyes, his smile, his lips. His hands and body. She imagined him out on the waters, strong as he pulled up nets full of fish in the early morning light. At midmorning, she imagined him making deliveries from house to house with Santino and became excited by guessing at what moment he would be pausing at the waterside entrance of the House of Orso. In the afternoons, she tried to imagine how a young fisherman done with his work might busy himself. Was he making a meal of roasted clams and bread, soon to nap in a sunny courtyard? Was he mending nets to the squawking of seabirds upon the sands of the lagoon? Perhaps he studied the mandolin and took pleasure in strumming out songs with those rough fingers. Or maybe he simply enjoyed watching the comings and goings of the merchant ships from a window overlooking the sea. Who was to know? She wondered if he'd thought about her, even once, after that day they had met in the kitchen. She wished that she might see him again, and one evening, was wholly surprised about the way she actually did.

Orso relished music and revelry, frequently
hosting robust masquerades to entertain fellow nobles
and their families. Fortunately, he had a wife who
knew how to plan a lavish feast. On the days
surrounding a fete, additional cooks and servants were
temporarily hired to ensure the perfect preparations.
Boats full of vegetables, game, fish, and flowers were
delivered to the *palazzo* and the home was clamorous
with the beating of rugs, sweeping of stones, and
polishing of pewter. It was always exciting for Mafalda
and her sisters as they anticipated what should be
worn and whom they might meet on those dreamlike
evenings. And though noble daughters were carefully
watched, the rules were loosened during those
illustrious nights when even Orso and his wife danced,
gambled and feasted into the early morning hours. Of
course, vendors were invited to deliver many times
more than their usual loads, and men like Santino and
his son would have known well in advance, the feast
plans of many of Venice's noble houses.

"Mistress." A man said, bowing low before her on
one such night.

Mafalda had been surprised. Though every guest
went disguised, she could recognize a great many

people by their manner and voice. For those she did not know, proper introductions were made. She neither recognized this man, nor had she been lately introduced to him. But when he stood, and she saw the smirk on the man's lips, she realized that she was mistaken. An introduction *had* been made, on an afternoon when apricot and crumbs could be found on her lips. The pearl from that day, already clasped in gold, now hung from her elegant neck.

Mafalda swallowed nervously, feeling thankful to be wearing a mask. "Sir? Do I know you?"

The half-mask that covered just her eyes sparkled in the firelight of the great hall. Her dark-blond hair was bound and pinned, some beautiful loose swirls creating a fall over one shoulder. Tonia had pulled the strings of her bodice with added force that night, accentuating her slim waist, and the shelf of her soft bosom where the pearl hung. Ample skirts flowed about her legs while her delicate feet smarted in heeled slippers that pinched.

Everywhere around them pulsed a great energy. By pipe, string and tambourine, the music played to make the dancers jump and turn. Mafalda could hear her father bellowing in some far corner, while much other laughter echoed through the hall to the clinking of metal and glass. No one sat to table all at once, as would happen at a more intimate dinner. Rather, guests wandered haphazardly around the feast, eating when and what they pleased. There, one snatched up basted meat while here, a handful of roasted nuts or a piece of sweet ripened fruit was enjoyed. Servants scurried about the room, filling empty goblets and bringing fragrant new dishes as they became ready.

"Hmmm." He sighed, pondering how best to answer her question. "You cannot have forgotten me so soon, for I see my gift hangs like a star upon the heavens of your breast."

Only moments had so far passed between them, yet with just one sentence, this man of the sea had unraveled her. She swallowed hard, her bosom beginning to rise and fall as quick as a sparrow's downy chest. But though she was nervous, she smiled for him and said his name.

"Baldovino." She liked how it sounded to say aloud. "But how came you to be here?"

He immediately understood her question and could not be offended by it. He was but a fisherman and a hawker, not likely to be invited to a feast in such a fine house, no matter how respected he and his father might be. But of course, he would not hide the truth from her.

"I came to be here through the door I always use, for there was no other way open to me to gain access to you." Their closeness compelled Baldovino to reach out and gently caress a strand of Mafalda's hair between his fingers, but he quickly pulled his hand back again. Anyone might be watching.

Just then, Mafalda caught sight of Paola, who gamboled through the crowd right past them. The youth flashed a smile at her sister, which was accompanied by a flickering look of approval, and then slipped out of sight. Paola was quiet and would never ask about this stranger. Even though she was the youngest, and the youngest tended to be the most curious, Paola's inquisitiveness was for the world rather than for indulgent gossip. Mafalda admired her for her reticent nature, even whilst wishing she and her sisters were closer confidants. She quickly drew her attention back to Baldovino.

"Does Martinella know?" She whispered.

"Yes, sweet lady. Without her, I would never have made it past the larder." He reached out again, smoothing a finger over the skin of her wrist.

They were playing with fire. But in that moment, when she soon felt the touch of his hand glide over her own, all she could think of was the pleasure. The pleasure she'd get out of the words he might deliver. The pleasure she'd receive with each forbidden touch. The pleasure she now felt just knowing that he'd gained access to the banquet in search of her. She was excited to have made any impression strong enough that he would take such a risk. There was also the simple pleasure of just his standing within her reach, his body warming hers in spite of the judicious distance between them.

"Well then sir, will you dance?" She asked, taking hold of his wandering hand.

As their bodies moved together through the pressing crowd, she knew that it was just the beginning. She hoped there would be many more such stolen moments in the future. She could not have known that they would in fact be repeated with impassioned consistency. But such meetings can only satiate for an hour, perhaps a day, ever leaving lovers wanting more. And so eventually becoming brazen, they took more, and conceived.

Mirella

"Speak ghost, and tell me why you have come." She managed, her body trembling as she watched Lagia in the shadows aside Orso's painting.

The figure laughed, a human laugh, scratchy and deep. "I am no ghost, Mirella. Though I will soon be one." Lagia looked upon the portrait once more, admiringly. "And where is your husband? I've not heard his voice carrying through the halls, and what great echoing halls they are! It is a fine palace, and *you* the queen of it."

It seemed impossible, but it *was* her sister. As the woman walked toward her, Mirella backed away from the door and out into the chamber. Lagia emerged from the closet and scanned the room with wonder. The fine furniture, large comfortable bed, expensive wall hangings and general roominess would have proved grand in her eyes. What would it have been like to live in a nunnery for more than twenty years, one's room a cramped, sparse, drafty cell? By the looks of it, such accommodations had aged her sister exceedingly. But as Mirella reviewed Lagia's costume, her clothes did not look like those of a simple nun. Back over her shoulders hung the long blue cloak, dirty and worn. At her front was exposed a threadbare dress with an obscenely low neckline, a discolored chemise peeking out.

For a fleeting moment, Mirella considered Mafalda's open chamber door. If Mafalda had not fled the *palazzo*, then why was her portal ajar and who had coughed from that direction? She'd have walked there straightaway to see what was amiss, but for the unfathomable presence before her.

"Lagia." She gasped, as if just realizing it was truth, and that she had not yet greeted her relative with civility. "Dearest Lagia, sister. How have you come to be here? I...I had a letter that you...the plague. Oh Lagia, this is all too disquieting. Are you quite well? Hadn't you the plague?"

The last question frightened her to consider. If Lagia had had the plague, she could have brought it here. Mirella looked over her sister's spoiled garments with suspicion. All clothing and possessions of those infected were to be scrupulously burned. Lagia's gown didn't look as though it had been washed in some time.

"A letter of my death? This *is* sad, sister. But nay, the letter spoke not of me." Lagia's face broke away from the awe she was so clearly experiencing while looking upon riches, and became somber. "I did not know this myself. Nay no, it was not me. It was our half-sister, Imilia."

"How now? I know of no sister named Imilia! And the letter contained no signature. Did *you* write the letter, Lagia? Is this some scheme?" She felt suddenly that she must sit down, exceedingly confused and exhausted by this surprise. "Forgive me. Come Lagia. Sit down with me and tell me how you have made your way to Venice."

Lagia smiled wearily, though with an artful hint. "Will you not first embrace me Mirella? Your sister? Are you not happy to see me?"

Mirella swallowed hard, terrified to do so. The plague. "I am. But you have shocked me and I must sit. Come. Take your ease before the fire. I will pour us some wine."

Mirella hoped her fast excuse would be enough. She could not touch her. She would later smash the glass she drank from, and burn the cushions Lagia sat upon, once her sister was safely gone. However, she would not send her away without first hearing how and why she had made it to the House of Orso.

Lagia moved over to one of the chairs set before the fire and sunk into its plush comfort. As Mirella made her way closer to gather glasses and pour the wine, she got a better look at her sister's face in the fire's glow. The sun had now fully set and the firelight flickered about the room. There, not only could she see a face tired and distressingly worn, but also one with blistering sores around its lips and a wretchedly blackened eye. Mirella had never gone near to anyone with the plague, but these wounds were hardly the sign of pestilence. If it were the scourge, Lagia's sores would be large and excruciatingly tender. And in a fevered condition, she would neither be able to speak nor stand. She would have been in a deathly state, incoherent. The signs were not even such that Mirella suspected her of recently having the contagion. Nevertheless, Mirella gingerly handed her sister a glass goblet, careful that their fingers should not touch with its passing.

Lagia slumped back in her chair as though she'd sat there many times before, as though she were the mistress of the room. Her manners were far less graceful than Mirella remembered, especially as she took long and lusty gulps of wine, emptying her glass. Mirella filled it full once more, and then sat down beside her.

As Lagia took in the fire, she asked again, "And Orso, *your* husband, is he not here?"

"No. He is not. Orso is dead. Several months gone. We believe it was the plague." She said matter-of-factly.

"Oh Mirella!" Lagia uttered, looking up from the fire with solemnity. "I am *so* sorry. So sorry for your girls. They are all women now, no? The youngest, fifteen?"

Her girls? The youngest fifteen? Mirella's back became rigid. This was curious. How had Lagia learned of her daughters? She'd never accepted a single letter in the nunnery from their brother. How could she have discovered the births of her nieces?

"I don't understand. Who told you news of my daughters? And, who is this Imilia? Lagia, how have you come to be here?" Mirella had gone from shocked, to wary, to angry. What emotions would come next? What was she about to hear?

Lagia grimaced with what looked like a flash of pain. But in an instant, the expression was gone. It was evident that she *was* ill, but with what? A smile reappeared on her face, a grimace burgeoning beneath it.

"How do *I* know about your daughters?" She paused, glancing at the fire and then slowly turning back to Mirella. "Because it was *I* who gave birth to them all."

Mirella rose to her feet abruptly, instantly dropping her goblet to the floor. But the sound of shattering glass was dull in her ears, so full were they with the cottony black echo of panic that circulated throughout her body. She clutched her chest and gasped, looking with wild eyes upon her sister. Never had she received such a blow in all her life.

Paola

Paola woke up in a strange place. The air around her was bitingly cold and her toes felt stiff and frigid. A snatch of moonlight flooded in though a high window lined with iron bars, and quietly glowed upon a barren stone wall and floor. As her eyes adjusted to being awake, her body began to fill with cool dread and loneliness. She now remembered where she slept, darkly alone, in her small cell, restless on one slim creaky cot. A terrible thought came to her. *This is forever.*

She wanted to cry. She wanted someone familiar to rush in through that forbidding wooden door in the wall, that portal between her and one silent, hopeless hall lined with prisoners' cells. She began to feel desperate as she stared at the ominous stony ceiling. She felt claustrophobic, as though the stones might fall down on her, and trap her in this place for eternity. These overwhelmingly desolate feelings, slipping over her in the dead of night, were powerful enough to drive someone to hysteria.

With how distressed she felt after just a few days in the nunnery, she was sure she could not comprehend the despair city criminals felt when abandoned indefinitely to their cells. Always dark, damp and suffocatingly hot in summer. Tormentingly glacial in winter. They starved, became diseased, went mad. She imagined they'd been utterly euphoric when the plague struck Venice, released to undertake the business of the dead. What fear could a man have of the plague, when he had already lived in Hell?

Of course, her situation was not so bad as that, but she would need to *find* a way to cope. In their own cells, lining this hall, were plenty of others. Some much older, some just a little, and a few which were even younger than she. There were ways to survive, perhaps even to thrive. She pondered such things to try and comfort herself. There was fellowship, filled with conversation, games and laughter. She could share that with the other nuns, she would make friends! Then there was the work of one's hands. Paola could learn to embroider well, to strum heavenly music upon an instrument or offer it up with practiced song. She could learn to cook good things for her fellow nuns, or master the tending of the earth in the convent garden. But would any of that ever be enough? Could it ever be as sweet as freedom? Would she ever stop feeling as alone as she did right now, or would this grow worse? There was one thing she knew. She had something pressing on her, drawing her even deeper into the darkness, and she wanted to be free of it.

Each night, a high nun sat outside in the long hall to keep an eye on the doors. Paola was told that seeking her out in the night should be reserved for urgent matters, only if she should take ill, or needed to make a critical confession. In that case, she could exit her room and plead her case to the night-watch nun. If this privilege were abused, her door would be locked each evening, accentuating those feelings of entrapment that came with each setting sun. Why was there a guardian, when escape out of the convent was difficult, unlawful, and with safety outside highly unobtainable? Their families had given them up, and there was little protection elsewhere. Another youth had whispered to Paola that it was because some nuns in their loneliness sought out the nightly comforts and warmth of other nuns, which was considered a great sin. This was a novel thought for Paola.

With bare feet in the darkness, she padded her way over to the door and opened it wide enough to stick her head out. Candles were dispersed along the hall, marked at intervals to light the way. As she captured the high nun's attention with a gentle whisper, a woman who looked to be praying fervently for daylight, Paola thought better than to make her confession. What if she was taken from the nunnery at sunrise and strung up from the gallows? But as the nun, old and wiry, slowly stood from her hard cedar chair, Paola was resolved to release her pain once and for all.

"Yes, my child. What draws you from your peaceful slumber?" The nun blinked calmly.

The woman's soft wrinkles and slight frame reminded Paola of Martinella. If only it were her, her sweet companion and friend, to unburden her secret to.

"I...I have a confession. It is dire." She explained in a mutter.

"I see. But you are new here, no? Took you not confession with the priest on the day of your arrival? Did you not reveal all of your sins when seeking this sanctuary?" The nun asked unemotionally. She appeared accustomed to dealing with excited girls, new to the nunnery.

"All but one sin. The worst sin of all my sins." Paola tried her best not to cry, though the unavoidable tears began to pool in her eyes.

"But the priest is with the dying, and their confessions are more urgent than yours." The nun tilted her head, chiding even as her aged face went on expressionless.

In other times, Paola would have assumed the dying to represent the most ancient, or sickly nuns among them, but in these times, she was almost certain that it was the plague.

"But this is why it is even more important that I confess. The pestilence is everywhere. I must make confession. May I share it with *you*?" She asked sincerely, a flicker of hopefulness in her pleading.

"No. If it is still so important a confession at sunrise, you may speak to the priest then. To wait out the hours, I suggest speaking to God yourself through prayer." With that, the high nun cut off any new appeal, wearily turning and shuffling back to her chair, resuming her own prayers.

After closing the door, Paola moved to the center of the room and into the only bit of light there was from the moon's silvery rays. There in her shift, feet bare and icy with the cold emanating from below, ebony hair loose, and shaking with chill, she clasped her hands and confessed, begging for forgiveness. It was she. She had made herself sick with wolf's bane purchased in the market. A poisonous plant sold for its medicinal qualities when administered in meager doses. It was easily accessible, yet purportedly used more often for villainous purposes rather than for healing. It was also she who poured the extract into Tonia's pewter tankard. But why? Paola had been emotionally weak and confused, impatient with feeling unloved. She'd desperately wanted attention. She'd only meant to make herself a little sick, hoping that her mother would finally feel compelled to offer her even a little affection. But unfortunately, while in her poisoned state, Mirella still had not shown her any love or compassion, the motherly attention she so needed.

But why feed the poison to Tonia, an innocent handmaiden (albeit meanly jealous and a thief)? When she'd spied Tonia taking her treasures, peeking in from a crack in her door, she became territorial and wanted to teach Tonia a lesson. Those pilfered items were either cherished gifts from her parents, or precious pieces from exotic places she yearned to see one day but knew she never would. Of course, Tonia had only been envious, but Paola had her own deep envies. She envied any daughter ever cherished by their mother. Didn't even Tonia have a mother who loved her and worried for her? How lucky, yet here she was snatching up what little comforts Paola had, including some few things Mirella had given her.

But now, she was very sorry. She'd only meant to make Tonia a little sick too, but delivered more poison into that cup than she'd realized. She now desperately wished that she could go back, never to have bought the aconite. She would befriend the maid, share with Tonia, who'd only stolen out of her own bitterness. How could Paola have slain that young woman? How had she been so craftily capable of lying about the source of her own illness? And after it all, she'd allowed Tonia to take the blame from where she slept in her grave. Unfathomable acts. Her soul was unlikely to be redeemed after such crimes. Could Tonia hear her, forgive her? Would God? Could confession, regret and prayer ever make her pure again?

Weary with her spiritual toil in the cold light of the moon, she eventually moved back to her pallet and fell exhausted into the scratchy woolen cloak that now provided her added warmth atop her paltry coverlet. But there she could not fall asleep, thinking continually of her soul.

Martinella

I.

When Mirella had arrived in Venice to take her place in the House of Orso, Martinella was silently suspicious that the young woman had lost a seed of the womb. Though a fresh bride, she avoided her husband's bed for several weeks. It could have been the fatigue of her first travels from her father's home. It could have been the adjustment to a new place and position. It could have even been shyness to the marriage bed. But Martinella knew better. Mirella, in the quiet of her chamber, showed melancholy. Her linens were spotted here and there with blood, for far longer than menses lasted. She'd been commonly tired and had slept much. And especially in those first few days, she'd been pale and her face continually damp.

Looking back on this memory, Martinella remembered how hard the woman had tried to cover up her difficulties during those weeks. Though near collapse when in her private room, having requested of her husband a little time in separate chambers until she felt ready to receive him, she was still charming and full of vigor in the dining hall before him each evening. She laughed, she danced, she ate, and she smiled for Orso.

Soon enough she was well, became his bedded wife, and shared a room with her husband. And as far as Martinella had known, no one had ever whispered any suspicion. Not one of the servants, which was unique. She doubted that even Orso had understood what had happened. His wife had been attentive and beguiling in the great hall as they'd feasted each night, and so he'd allowed her the time she'd asked for to adjust to the *palazzo*, behaving far more civilized than any other man who had ever won such a beautiful prize. And so, with no whisperings about, Martinella believed she was the only one who'd known. She had wondered whose the child had been. If Orso and the lady had consummated their union before taking their vows, then it would have been unnecessary for Mirella to act quite as she did just after her arrival. There must have been another man there first. But this business did not concern her, and so she pushed the mystery deep and away.

As the months went on, Mirella's belly never grew with new child. Such conceptions were always the delight of fresh noble marriages. Other stately wives shared advice on how to most quickly conceive, for it was vitally important for a noble wife to deliver a healthy, hearty heir as soon as possible. Servant women also encouraged new wives with merry singing and happy thoughts.

> *Aye mistress, soon you'll bear a goodly son! Think you now! What shall we serve at the feast? How proud your husband will be! Aye mistress, think ye now of what to name your firstborn, for soon you will be full with child!*

Very early in the marriage, Martinella could see that the lady had fallen deeply in love with her husband. She too, must have been hopeful to make their bond lasting with children. But in spite of year after year of coupling, they never did conceive. Martinella sometimes wondered if it hadn't something to do with the woman's health those first weeks. Had the young woman's loss prevented her from ever becoming pregnant again? Had the episode damaged her womb? It was all too possible. But even before it was entirely certain to Martinella that Mirella could not make children, the lady of the house became a mother nevertheless. However, the world never knew that the baby had not been hers.

The couple annually traveled to Treviso in the coldest season, to celebrate religious holidays and dance their feet upon *terra firma*. Occasionally too, they traveled together during the warmer months. On four such pilgrimages, their return had been months delayed. This was not strange, for nobles traveled away and for long bouts, just as they pleased. But at the end of those extended occasions, Mirella returned with a babe in her arms. The household was overjoyed, the nobles congratulated, and feasts were held. It was *especially* exciting, for no one had known that the couple was expecting! How sly for them to travel away for Mirella's lying-in! But Martinella knew better. Peculiarly, the babes *did* resemble their mother's looks and manners as they grew, but this could only have been coincidence. She knew, as any old woman who had lived many years in the world knew, that Mirella had never labored with child. But of course, she never uttered a word.

Though she had only been seeking to save herself from a life of enclosure, she quickly found herself in love with her husband, making it even more imperative that she secure her place. Without a child, Orso could seek to annul their marriage, and take a different wife in time. Mirella still wasn't entirely saved from a future in a nunnery.

Many a morning before she washed and dressed, she inspected her body in a tall mirror, one very expensive gift from her husband. She'd touch her belly, willing it to grow.

But every month she bled, no matter how many nights she lay with her husband. Her continued barrenness began to fill her with dread. What if the illness she had endured after losing Remo's child now prevented her from ever conceiving in future? What if her past sins now poisoned her future?

For five years, life went on in this way. Her love for her husband deepening while continually fearing that she could lose her place beside him if she did not give him a child. Orso could feel the tenderness in her love, and had loved her back, perhaps even more ardently. And though she never once revealed her hurts at not yet having conceived, he could see her flinch at news of other Venetian births.

The noble women of Venice were snickering. She could feel it; her ears were burning. Some even reproached Mirella over her empty womb. Perhaps she wasn't tempting her husband often enough? Was she eating the right foods? Was she getting enough rest? Had she prayed hard enough to be blessed? And though other noblemen would have begun to felt disdain for their wives, Orso did not. If her body could not carry a child, it was God's will. If she could not conceive, there were legions of infants in need of mothers. He would find one for her. He would give her a baby out of love and would offer the child his name, and his wife would be happy. It would be a sign of his devotion to her. She would see that he did not fault her, and that he had no intention of

Veleno

abandoning her.

II.

When a squalling Fina was placed in her arms, bald and immobile in her fine lacy swaddling, Martinella kissed the baby's soft cheeks nearly twenty times. The infant's sleepy eyes grew wide with such attentions until the serving woman swayed her back to sleep in the safety of her arms with a gentle hum. Alone with the child as she lay the baby down in a wide basket lined with richly embroidered cloth, she wished with a whisper over the slumbering girl.

"May you be bold and clever, precious Fina. Pray you seek out your own happiness in life, never to learn of the sorrows that come with bending to any will but your own. Be you brave, and unafraid!" Martinella chuckled with happiness as the baby cooed her promise.

The scene was shocking and unexpected, in spite of her having fully understood Venice's plight. She'd spied countless bodies lying in wait to be removed all along the canals, had to careen past them as she scurried through the narrow calli. She'd pressed one hand firmly over her mouth, trying hard not to cry out in awe and despair. At first light, she'd stolen away from Frosino's palace, leaving a letter for her courtesan friend. She was going back to the house, was seeking out solitude so that she could better consider her future. She would keep watch over Aurelia's home and bide time until times were better. Aurelia would understand.

The lock upon the waterside door had been found broken, and the door shut tightly behind some intruder, locked from within. Fina understood that she might encounter a dangerous guest if she went inside. Perhaps a rabid plunderer, a plagued castaway seeking shelter, or a demented derelict moving from off the streets into an abandoned house to live like a noble. She knew that it was dangerous to go in alone, but what choice did she have? Where else could she go? She could only hope that the trespasser had already come and gone as she used˙her iron key to gain entry by another door.

Fina could never have imagined that she was about to discover a sister inside, so changed from physical torment. From the very moment she stumbled upon the gaunt, pale body lying on the kitchen floor with a bloodied knife so near, she could only believe that a high and holy hand had been guiding her, for she had arrived only just in time to save her sister's fleeting life. She immediately worked to drag Mafalda up from the floor, up the stairs, and into her bed. Her sister was of little help, delirious after butchering her own foot.

As she ran back down to fetch up and boil water, Fina

was grateful to have listened to her own voice that morning. Had she not abandoned Frosino's gilded hospitality, guided by her own will rather than by any other consideration, it might not just have been too late for her sister, but also for herself. She would have been made fixed, permanent in one role or other that she was still apprehensive to undertake. Ever after that, she never forgot to listen to the voice inside her.

III.

When Mafalda was two years old, she'd been even more difficult than other children her age to keep watch over. One moment the girl would be attempting to climb a wobbly stool to get a peek out over the square. The next, she could be found clumsily running headfirst into a table or inching uncertainly down a marble stair. Martinella considered it a sort of miracle when the girl made it to the age of three without having met with some terrible accident. She was the sort of foolhardy child that made the entire household grit their teeth, gasp and get the nerves.

One afternoon while at that tender age, Mafalda had toddled away from Mirella, who was busy looking over a merchant's attractive, lustrous fabrics in the great hall. The girl moved too close to the hearth in the room and her dress caught fire. Hearing Mafalda's cries, Mirella ran to slap out the flame with her bare hands. Both of her palms had been burned, as well as the child's leg. While Mirella tended to her own wounds, Martinella dressed Mafalda's. The child had lost all her energy with the fright of what had happened, and lay whimpering and fevered in her bed. A burn, even the smallest of burns, was a very painful thing. Martinella wished that she could take away that pain, but could only do her best to clean the wound and make the child comfortable. As the serving woman carefully pinched away a bit of charred fabric from the child's leg, now red and peeling, the baby grimaced, whining piteously.

L'acqua, she'd asked when the cleaned burn was bound, pleading for a drink of water. Bringing a pewter cup to the baby, Mafalda sat up and gulped until she drank it all, and then fell back again, sighing and whimpering quietly for hours more. Seeing the child hardly alert and in such discomfort, Martinella prayed over her.

"God grant this child the strength to live past pain and suffering. Though she be burned, let her not be afraid of fire. With any scar, let strength be given, and may the Lord keep watch over her. Amen."

With outstretched hands and a faint smile, Mafalda handed over the emptied bowl of broth and then sunk back down into the soft bolsters supporting her back. Fina's arrival had been the greatest blessing she'd ever received in her life thus far. Though it had been an excruciating business for Mafalda, Fina had made her bite upon a thick stick from out of the kindling pile as she washed, stitched and bound her toes. It had now been two days since the horrible surgery. With Fina's constant attentions, the wounds were healing. Thankfully too, no fever had surfaced.

Fina solemnly asked what they should do with the amputated toes. Should they bury them in the home's modest, walled-in courtyard when Mafalda was better? Mafalda had laughed, but also with tears in her eyes for the terrible pains she had suffered. She was still going to have to figure out how to walk once her foot was healed. She might need a wooden staff, but that was nothing. She was alive!

Mafalda worried that Fina might become ill by tending to her when she had so recently had the plague. But Fina would not listen to a word her sister mumbled, working hard to help her get well again and entertaining her with stories. Fina could say that she'd been a courtesan for one night, even though she was yet a maid. The sisters laughed together with the telling. She also shared her surprising proposal. Of course, it had not been a serious declaration, but in the future it might be. Let them meet again under different circumstances once the plague subsided and see what direction their hearts might bend. Fina had seen much in Mondin that was worthy, but now wasn't the time for courtship.

As she mended in bed, Fina sitting beside her, the fire full and healing, Mafalda in turn revealed her affair with

259

Baldovino, and about the child she suspected was now growing in her belly. She sincerely feared that the babe might be marred by her terrible illness. She cried, and sobbed more as she revealed Paola's danger, Zeta's taking ill, the black night she'd been carried out of the palazzo after falling sick, and all that had transpired once she woke. She even told her about the dream in the pit, and what part Fina had played in it to alert her of her danger.

Fina was dumbfounded by all that she heard, nearly disbelieving that such an odyssey had taken place, but knowing that every word was true. She was deeply pained to learn of the things she had been absent for, while she'd been trying her hand at survival in her own way. Certainly Fina had thought about her family both night and day after leaving home, but what could she have done for any of them had she stayed? Mafalda, seeing the anguish on Fina's face, patted her sister's hand and thanked her for being there for her in that cold grave.

"But I wasn't there. I haven't been there for you, any of you, for a long time." Fina shook her head with distress, taking on the burden of an eldest child.

"But you were there, in strength and spirit when I needed you most." Mafalda assured. "And now, you can make me a promise. Be by my side the day my child comes. I'll need your strength then too."

Fina began looking around the room, scanning the floors and glancing at the feet of a writing desk.

"What are you looking for?" Mafalda asked, nervously studying the room.

"The knife you used to cut off those toes! It served you well. We'll put it under your bed the day the baby calls you to deliver. It will slice away the pain!" Fina chortled.

Mafalda grinned with her sister's teasing. It brought them both to laugh, and cry, until it hurt. It also brought a little healing to their hearts.

IV.

These were the prettiest children in Venice! So thought Martinella as she walked with Noemi at her side, aged 10, hand in hand on the way to the market. How precious they all were. Fina at 13 was already walking with a stately grace ahead of the rest. She would make an elegant lady. Mafalda at 12 chirped continuously, as pleasantly as a little bird. She would grow up to be a woman whom everyone enjoyed conversing with. And little Paola, so sweet and innocent at just 8, was ever curious about their path, there walking behind Mirella and trying to keep pace. The girl was concentrating hard on everything she saw with those dark eyes. That child reminded the old woman about inquisitiveness. As Paola looked up at a squawking seagull flying overhead, Martinella did too, and smiled. And then little Noemi, with her bobbing red curls beneath a white veil, with those silly faces she made and her frequent gasps of delight; she too was a charming child with spirit!

As the family walked along, through thin *calli* and over busy bridges on their way to the Rialto, Noemi stretched out a hand to touch every surface within reach; the marble of a church, the wooden banisters lining a bridge, the soft purple petals of dripping wisteria along a wall. And with the scent of a street vendor's roasting nuts, she cried, *Martinella! How delicious it smells!* The aged servant nodded with agreement. And as they passed workers cutting wood, and yelling loudly above their own cacophony as they mended an old building, the girl let go of Martinella's hand and threw hers up over her ears while looking over the scene with wonder. Noemi was a child sensitive to her surroundings, yet fascinated by her city.

Seeing Noemi's reaction, Martinella uttered inaudibly under the noise, but over the precious red head. "Saint Mark, blessed patron saint of *Venezia*, watch over this child for all of her days and guide this, a true child of Venice!"

Just then, Noemi drew her hands down from her ears and giggled. Beaming as she looked up at Martinella, she pointed out two laborers moving conscientiously together while carrying a large and priceless plaque of stained glass over a nearby bridge. The pieced image, artfully made, vibrant and proud, was that of a lion with wings standing over the Bible. It was the common symbol for Venice and its patron saint.

To what a sight had Ilario opened his door! As he ushered in the trembling woman, bedraggled and clutching a bloodied cross, she'd said not a word. But the look in her eyes said that she had seen and experienced much. Had she been hurt? What had transpired? Who had done this to her? But though instant fear and anger churned inside him, he did not wish to distress her with questions. He would tend to her maltreated body first, and wait for her distracted mind to catch up and use words.

He'd gently removed her cloak and had tenderly loosened the front strings of her bodice so that she could better breath. He'd sat her carefully before the fire and had removed her slippers, as gently as if she were but a vulnerable kitten. He'd heated water and had wiped down a swelling place upon her forehead and had gingerly cleaned the blood trickling from a cut there. He'd washed her face and neck, and had rinsed her hands with care in a soothingly warm bowl. He'd given her a heated cup of wine to sip, hoping it would help with some of the pain. He'd even gathered up her wild curls, and had inspected the bruises developing around her neck. And when her quivering ceased, and her body had been warmed, he'd led her up to his humble bed, where he laid her down, and where she fell asleep in his arms. Whichever way she shifted, he moved to hold her, keeping watch over her. He only fell asleep with the blue of the earliest morning light.

When she woke, a seabird crying loudly outside without regard to the distress Venice was already in, she'd almost forgotten where she was and where she had been. But as she sat up in the slender bed, she felt the soreness all throughout her body and saw the cuts and bruises on her hands, and it all came back. There beside her, Ilario slept. She watched him as his wide chest rose and fell steadily. But wait, a sudden cough stirred him. And also, there on his brow were small beads of sweat. Ilario woke, saw Noemi and smiled, and reached out to her, glad. But there, another cough and he pulled back his hand to cover his mouth. Could Ilario be sick?

In an instant, she was very much frightened. What if she were to lose him? He was the only safe place in her uncertain world and it would be unbearable to see him suffer. Her heart began to beat anxiously, while her face radiated an impenetrable seriousness amidst lawless red tangles. But then a miracle happened. Ilario sneezed forcefully, twice in a row, and then once again after a pause. This was no symptom of the plague. Ilario had a cold.

"God bless you." She whispered, before shifting low to kiss his damp head.

V.

Martinella had searched everywhere for Paola! The dance master had arrived for the girls' weekly tutorial with three hired musicians in tow, and she didn't want to keep them waiting. Such lessons were the luxury of the rich, and Mirella expected her four daughters to be able to dance as gracefully as any other noble girls in Venice. It was quite a matter of pride. As for Martinella, she simply liked that the girls laughed and received ample exercise, and were occupied and merry throughout their lessons. And though Paola enjoyed dancing as much as her sisters, she was the youngest and the most easily distracted, frequently forgetting the engagement. After some searching, she was regularly found in some far corner of the *palazzo*.

Out of breath, Martinella finally spotted her in Orso's meeting chamber. The door was wide open and the man himself could be heard snoring as loudly as a bear while napping in a comfortable chair under a window. The good light pouring in where he sat created an optimal time for reading, but Orso's book went abandoned. Paola sat alone at his table, strewn with wax-sealed letters, yellowing papers and dusty books. And there, just seven years old, she studiously attempted to copy with quill and ink, a faded map. Martinella was certain that this was the only girl in Venice to spend time at such tedious, odd hobbies. Studying and drawing maps! But perhaps it was not *too* strange, considering she was a Venetian and that Venice had the most powerful army of ships, explorers and merchants in the world! The desire for adventure had clearly sparked her nascent mind.

Martinella quietly entered the room and moved toward the girl, careful not to wake the master of the house. Standing before the table, Paola still did not look up, completely invested in etching the likeness of a foreign glob.

"Paola?" The serving woman whispered. "Have you forgotten the hour? You are late for your dance lesson. Tarry not, everyone awaits you."

The dark head peered up. A serious look showed on the girl's face, as though she had for some time been deep in thought. Slowly, she set the quill down and noiselessly pushed out her chair. Walking around the table, so gentle and meek that not a step was heard, she took up Martinella's soft wrinkly hand and they headed toward the door. When they were in the hall, she spoke.

"Martinella? My mother says that boys can sail the

sea, but that girls cannot. She says too, that men can be merchants, but that women can only be wives, or nuns. Is that true?" Paola's little hand squeezed the woman's with her question.

She was not certain how to answer. Though the child's spirits were made low by such a revelation, she didn't want to feed her false hopes just to try to raise them.

"Hmmm. What your mother says is true, I'm afraid. But consider, how dangerous and difficult such expeditions must be! Perhaps it is for our own good that we remain home, in Venice, where it is safe." Martinella wasn't satisfied with her own answer, but didn't know what else to say. This wasn't a topic she had thought much about. But certainly, a woman who desired it *should* be allowed the right to see the world as much as any man.

"But I wish to sail from Venice and see what lies beyond! To see the places painted on my father's maps." Paola frowned sincerely. "How might I do it, Martinella?"

Without a pause to think of the possible consequences, the woman's eyes smiled and she teased, "I suppose you could raze your pretty head, dress in the garments of a man, and go just where you like! But it would not be easy, and you would have to be very clever, for the world outside of Venice is as likely to be dangerous as it is sure to fascinate."

She instantly regretted saying this when she heard the gasp and saw the honest look of excitement on Paola's face. What if the girl asserted such a plan before her mother! That would not bode well for the serving woman. What if Paola took the idea too seriously and attempted to run away in childish pursuit. This was very unlikely, but children were surprising creatures.

"Nay, now. I am just an old woman who speaks foolishly!" She retracted.

"No, Martinella! How clever! I'd never thought of something like that..." Paola's feet hopped and her eyes were filled with possibility.

"Paola." She stopped them both in their steps. "You must never consider such a thing. At least, you must wait until you are a woman, and then decide where your heart calls you to go. I suspect that when you are grown, you may feel differently about leaving Venice, but we shall see. For now, study your father's maps and peruse the exotic wares of our merchants. But dwell not on these things so hard, that you forget to dance!"

Paola woke. Her black hair was damp with sweat, her body clammy beneath a warm blanket. The cheery beacon of a single candle, gone low and drizzling wax on a bedside table, stirred her to reality. Her confessions had only been another nightmare! How strange was the mind in sleep! Yes, she was still cocooned in her nunnery cell, but no, she had committed no murder, and had delivered no poison. She had committed no sin. She thanked her Heavenly Father. Two things however, had been true of the awful dream: that continual desire to know a mother's love, and her tenacious hope to see the world. Sitting up in her bed, she believed she might still have just one of those wishes fulfilled. But not while trapped here. She could not stay. She did not belong in a convent. But when and how would she make her escape? She would have to be patient, watch and wait for the right opportunity.

But as she leaned toward the table to blow out the candle, now a commodity she should not waste, she heard a terrible, muffled cry resonating through the stones. Paola felt a chill. Who could make such a cry, such a noise that it would carry through thick rock? Silence returned. Her cell was so quiet that she could make out the beating of her heart. But as she focused her listening, waiting for further noises from outside, the beating in her chest sounded as distinct as a fist's continual thumping in wet sand. And there it was again, a shocking scream from somewhere deep in the convent! Had someone needed surgery in the night? Perhaps it was a tooth gone rotten. She had heard that this could cause terrible agony. Paola hoped that it was some natural malady, and not what she most feared.

Allowing the diminishing candle to remain lit, she tried to lie back in her bed for a time, but continued to hear the pained call. After the tenth or twelfth scream, Paola could stand the silence between each howl no longer. Getting out of bed, barefoot in her shift and damp hair falling over her shoulders, she toed to the door. Would it be open as in her dream, or was she locked in at night? She'd only been there a few days, hadn't ever tried the door after falling asleep. Holding her breath, she pulled. Though heavy, the door opened with ease and Paola peeked out into the hall.

A bit of light bloomed at intervals from sconces along the stone walls, but the way was dim. Quietly moving out from the door, she hesitantly walked through the shadows, her feet cold as she went. Where was the nun who kept watch? Maybe there wasn't one. If there was, she might fly down this hall from either direction, at any moment, and frighten Paola to death. She continued to move, not at all sure which way to walk, but needing to move forward nevertheless. How could every other woman here remain in her room with such crying? Not a single one was peeking out from their door, each portal shut tight.

Just then, beneath one dollop of candlelight, she spotted

a nun slumped over in a chair against the wall. Was she sleeping, or was she ill? It certainly wasn't the same woman who had been screaming, or else the cry would have sounded less muffled. Look at the sweat that glistened on her brow! Had she fainted? Was she alive? Had she the plague?

Paola panicked, abandoned the body and hurried down the hall as fast as she could. At a crossway, she had no knowing which way she should turn, and so chose right and kept going. If she could just keep moving, she could hold on to a thread of hope. The sconces that were lit grew fewer until there were no more alight along the path she followed. Her eyes adjusted to the darkness, but there was so little light, that she could hardly make out the path. Paola splayed her fingers out before her to protect herself and considered turning back to try another way.

But then she saw it, and remembered those awful dreams when back at home. She'd believed such strange visions had been the result of her poisoning, but considered now that the nightmares had been a sort of premonition. A large, dark shadow moved in the darkness before her. Her hair was damp and cool from sweat. Wearing only a shift, her feet were bare. It was just like the dreams. She stopped, stared into the darkness, and tried to focus on the bulk that was just out of view. It was then that she heard more screaming and groaning through the stone. Again, just like her dreams. Paola was very afraid.

She could turn back. She could run the other direction, or scurry back into her room. She didn't have to face what was lurking in the darkness. But what was worse? Certain death if she became exposed to the plague, or the uncertainty of what was before her? Paola, her heart beating like a rabbit's while fleeing a chase, continued forward. As she moved further and further along, her feet searching over the stones, the large shadow lingered before her, but just out of sight. Who was there? What was there?

Moments later, she found herself in a breezy spot. It must be another crossway, but it was so dark that she feared to move in any direction. Was this some place in the convent rarely used? Or was it just a place never traversed after dark, and thus no candles lit? The shadow shifted and she considered that the apparition must be all in her mind, her brain addled by weeks of stress. She wanted to scream, but was even too afraid of the darkness to do that. It was then that the slightest glow began to emanate from the place where the figure seemed to float, and she could finally see it for what it was.

"Papa?" She was completely bewildered, nearly shocked to stone.

Orso's enormous figure teetered before her in the shadows, lightly illuminated. He silently smiled, and then with an encouraging bellow, replied.

"Go you that way, daughter!" The man pointed left, the way vaguely lit with his light.

In an instant, the glow was gone. With it went Orso and the hovering presence he'd cast in the darkness. Paola could have fallen to her knees, wanted to sob and beg him back again until there was no more water and salt to empty from her eyes. But this was not the time. At her father's command, she fled. One hand reached forward while the other guided her way, feeling along the old stones. She moved on in this way for what felt like forever, passing further crossways and paths as she went in the labyrinth that was the ancient nunnery. Finally, she passed a cavernous room, and then two and three more that had no doors! Glancing inside, she found that each contained a handful of high windows. They were not striped with iron bars! Blessedly too, she could see the faint blue of a new dawn flooding in. Day was coming.

The dens looked communal, for reading, study, and stitching. How might she reach one of those windows up so high? Running into one of the rooms, she strained to push a heavy table against the wall, using all her might. She then hurried to place a chair up on it, and then balanced a stool on its seat. As she climbed, she prayed for enough height to reach the targeted window, smash its glass, and escape.

Veleno

Come what may on the other side, a broken ankle or a plunge into a canal, Paola was leaving the nunnery.

Lagia

The story was nearly impossible to believe, but Mirella knew that what Lagia spoke was truth. Their father Severiano had continually planted his seed outside of his marriage and everyone, including his wife, was aware of it. He was not the sort of man to hide his infidelities. Of course, children had been born out of some of those illicit romps. But to learn of a half-sister named Imilia, and how she secretly took Lagia's place in the nunnery, was surpassingly surprising.

Lagia never learned exactly how old Imilia had been when they'd met. The young woman had displayed youthful mannerisms, but a difficult life belied her bloom. Lagia believed she might have been about one of their ages, hers or Mirella's. Wearing old tattered clothes and worn leather shoes, with her hair hanging in grimy strands and much dirt beneath her fingernails, Lagia had spied the female stealing grapes from their family's vineyard. Feeling sorry for her, so evidently hungered and desperate-looking, she could not bring herself to reproach the woman. After all, she too was feeling hopeless, albeit in a different way entirely. Mirella and Orso had just been wed, and Lagia would soon be sent away forever. She'd quietly approached the young woman, and had used soft words so as to not frighten her away.

Showing great gentleness toward the lady, it didn't take long for Lagia to ascertain her story. Imilia's mother had died, and she had no other family at all. There was no one in the world to take care of her. Despairing, she'd walked a great distance to partake of her *father's* table, in whatever way she could. Imilia's mother had spoken of Severiano twice or thrice. But with those words, Imilia had clearly understood that she was illegitimate, and that her birth had held no importance to her father.

Her mother, Cadiana, had been a laundress for the nearest local public house. The work was backbreaking and paid very little, but she was provided with a cramped room of her own in the drafty attic. In the worst of times, Imilia's mother would cry over her blistered hands and pray aloud for a husband to come and care for them. And giving Imilia the greater share of their paltry table, Cadiana always looked alarmingly thin, and could hardly bear her work. No husband ever came, for she was not a maid and everyone knew her child had come by Severiano. Men were not only wary of *him*, but also of marrying any woman who had so eagerly and outwardly sinned.

Who could have known that the laundress hadn't willingly gone to bed with Severiano? When he'd grabbed her, she'd been too shocked and frightened to deny a noble, and had not fought him off. It had been on a spring evening after a great hunt. Severiano and a band of men had dined and taken rooms in the public house. Imilia's mother had then been young, pretty, and a virgin. He'd watched her delivering fresh linens into his room, and had decided to take advantage. This single union had been painful for Cadiana, was to give her a daughter, and would also be her doom. If only she'd had the courage to fend him off and escape his dangerous grip! But fear was an inconstant power, giving strength to some while arresting others. When her belly began to grow, she'd felt such guilt, but Cadiana's sweet soul was in every way, blameless.

When Severiano spotted the pretty laundress in the village seven months later, toiling to get water from the well, struggling with her round belly, he'd laughed. She'd caught sight of his wicked reaction to her wearying exertions, and for the very first time in her innocent heart, a deep, black hate had stirred within. However, at least his seeing her condition forever spared her from being sought out again. Nonetheless, even after witnessing his scorn, she had secretly hoped that he might send her a little money. Now and then, for his child? But Severiano never did.

As Imilia grew, she'd spot her father in the town every now and again. Cadiana had never kept his identity from her. Everyone knew anyway. When her mother had stumbled out of Severiano's room that fateful night, the proprietress had seen her. And by the time the young woman's belly grew, the truth had long circulated. Imilia had never had the courage to approach him, fearing what would happen if she ever did. He might laugh at her, or even strike her for her insolence. This was what titled, moneyed noblemen sometimes did. How commanding was his walk, and how dark the look in his face! For all of this, Imilia had always kept her distance. And even though she should have hated him as much as her mother, she sometimes could not help but to create a tender thought for him. After all, he was still her father.

But now, Imilia could remain at a distance no longer. When her mother died, work-worn and weak-lunged, Imilia hadn't been given her mother's place as the inn's laundress. Neither had any man in the village shown signs of an honest affection for her. If they had, she would have married any one of them without question, for without shelter, what would become of her? Dispelled from her attic room to make way for the new tenant, Imilia did the only thing she could think to do. She walked the miles from the village, hid in the vineyard, and planned her approach to the estate. She would not ask Severiano for help, but would instead beg his steward for work, any work the lands or villa might have. When Lagia had come across her, she'd already been sleeping in the vineyard for three consecutive nights. Imilia had been living entirely off of the grapes, which was certain to have been disturbing to the young woman's bowel.

With the discovery of this half-sister in the vineyard, Lagia conceived a knotty plan that could offer them both hope. Might Imilia consent to take Lagia's place in the convent? It was not freedom, but it was a permanent home and safety, and she would never go hungry again. It seemed impossible that any young woman would consent to such a plan, but Imilia did, eagerly committing to the scheme.

Lagia led Imilia to a safer place to hide. She would have to live outside for just a few days more, near a gentle stream protected by a length of thicket. Lagia also brought her a cloak and food so that she would not be too uncomfortable. Finally on the night before Lagia was to leave for the nunnery, she snuck Imilia into her chamber. The lady had had to climb a wall of thorns and vines. Though breathless and bleeding, she'd tumbled silently in through the window. There in the night, Imilia bathed out of a chilled basin, ate her last meal outside of enclosure, dressed, and waited for dawn. Of one thing Lagia made Imilia promise; she should send back every missive, unopened, that ever was to find its way to her in the nunnery. Imilia said that she could not read or write in any case, and so the agreement was an easy one.

When Lagia's door opened at sunrise, Severiano, their brother Liborio, and some close servants stood by to watch as a veiled woman walked from the room, immediately to be delivered in a humble wagon to the convent. Lagia went unmoving in a wardrobe until all went quiet, some half an hour or more, and then scurried down the wall of vines with the very same urgency in which Imilia had climbed them.

With the aid of a small sack of coins and some gems to pawn, Lagia eventually made her way from Padua to Treviso. There, she carefully avoided men while humbly approaching women. Had they any idea where she might seek work? Why yes, a certain inn needed a laundress. Though uncanny, Lagia found her way to the inn. She soon learned that a small closet furnished with a pallet was also provided as lodging. She counted her blessings. This was sustenance and a shelter, temporarily at least until she could make some higher plan.

Lagia had never worked a day before, but quickly mastered her duties while doing her very best to remain sanguine. For even in her new toil, she yet had some valuable treasures at her disposal that could provide a sizeable sum whenever the need arose. Unfortunately, the innkeeper's wife had been suspicious of Lagia since the moment she knocked on their door for work. This young lady was too delicate, too well-spoken to be just another wayfaring farm girl in need of a position. Thus, one afternoon when Lagia sought a coin from her secret trove so that she could buy more victuals than her pay would allow, she discovered that her gems and money were missing.

This misfortune was grave, but she remained calm when reporting her loss, never divulging quite how much had been stolen. She didn't want to elicit too many questions, or someone might guess that she was in fact a noble's daughter. The innkeeper's wife had guffawed. Who in her inn would enter Lagia's room? Who would want to steal from a lowly laundress? What a tale to claim that she'd ever owned anything *worth* taking! Yet within the month, the building received enhancements that Lagia doubted the proprietors had money for, and grew certain that it had been the innkeeper's wife who had ruined her.

But how to legally accuse the fox without Lagia's identity being discovered? It was impossible. Uncertain of her safety if she were to leave with no gold at all, she continued on at the inn in spite of the theft. After some years had passed, continually half-starved on her meager salary, Lagia did what was once unthinkable. Now and then, she allowed a traveler into her room, for coin. The innkeepers seemed not to mind, for whatever pleased a guest, pleased their business. This was how over the years, Lagia had gotten five children: Fina, Mafalda, Noemi, Paola, and a son who was stillborn.

Each day that she'd carried the first child, Lagia had feared, for she knew that she could not care for a babe. Many precious hours of sleep were lost in worry. How could she maintain her position as a laundress, and still feed and care for a child? Then one night as she sat at one of the communal tables of the inn, nearly ready to give birth and chewing on abandoned chicken bones that were normally thrown to the dogs, she laid eyes on Orso. She rose from her table at once and went to him at his. He sent his men away and listened in astonishment, all the while sympathetic and tender towards her. This was a woman he once admired, and might have married, before his affections had moved to Mirella.

Orso wanted to give her money, but she refused. She may be poor and weary with hard labor, often going hungry, but she had chosen her path willingly and would let it take its course. Perhaps better fortune would yet find its way to her. However, in one thing she was not too proud. Entrusting the future of her child to his care. It was a frequent occurrence that men of fortune saw to the safety and upbringing of a ward. It was an easy thing and of little expense to send a babe to a caring farm family to be brought up. Many such families were glad for the extra income. Could he do this for her? He immediately assured her that he would. He'd see to the child's every comfort. It was the least he could do, having once abandoned a promise to her years before. She was relieved, though she could never have guessed that he'd intended to raise the child himself. He'd chosen to gift the baby to his barren wife. The daughter was raised as his own, and as a noble.

Though in her heart, it was wrong to take future men to her bed after losing her first child to someone else's care, bouts of desperation brought her to it. And as the births of three subsequent children approached, she wrote to Orso with a plea, and he came to claim each babe. How long Lagia had imagined her children wholesome and loved, each with a benevolent farmer family or the like. It wasn't until she'd overheard some of Orso's men, whom she recognized passing through Treviso to stay at the inn, that she learned of Orso's *four beautiful daughters*. She knew that they were not Mirella's, for Orso had once said that his wife went barren. So her sister not only enjoyed the husband she should have had, but was also raising Lagia's children as her own? This was painful and confusing news. But considering Lagia's *part* in Mirella's infertility, how could she embrace it as an injustice in her heart?

At this point in the admission, Mirella pressed Lagia to explain. What could possibly have been Lagia's role in Mirella's barrenness? What she confessed was unconscionable. Lagia had slipped an abortive poison to her *own sister* during Orso and Mirella's wedding breakfast before they departed for Venice. Lagia had heard Mirella's sickness through the door when she passed her chamber, and was certain her sister was pregnant, and that it was Remo's. However, it had not been for revenge that she had done something so criminal. Referencing their mother's old book of plants to help her, she'd concocted a dram primarily made of juniper berries. She was trying to *help* her sister, however much she'd hated her for stealing Orso. For if Mirella was so far gone with child to have the morning sickness, her new husband would soon become suspicious that the child was not his, and Mirella's marriage would be annulled. Lagia was trying to protect her. But who would have known that the poison would mare her, barring her from conceiving another child in the future? If that was in fact, why Mirella never became pregnant again.

But why had Lagia come now, Mirella wanted to know. How long had it been since she'd last seen Orso? *Many* years. She'd come because she was mortally sick with the great pox, syphilis, and was certain she hadn't long to live. This incurable illness had been gotten during the conception of her last babe, a boy. He'd been born without a breath, her disease most likely the cause. Beneath her dress were gruesome wounds that would not heal. At least she'd been spared it completely eating away at her face, as so often happened. With Heaven's gate daily opening an inch before her, she hadn't been afraid to leave Treviso, had not hesitated to travel, and had no fear of the plague.

She'd had to beg every step of the way for enough coin to complete the journey. With the pestilence all around, people had been very cautious, but some still gave. One man however, had hit her in the face, shouting for her to get away from him after spying a strange lesion on her chest. The fray had given her a bruised eye. But she'd made it. She just wanted to see her children once more before she was gone, and also to ask forgiveness from her sister.

"*Veleno.*" Mirella sighed as she studied Lagia's face; the sores around her lips now clear evidence of syphilis, and her aged appearance true signs of toil. "How our lives have been filled with *poison!*"

Before she could even begin to recover from all that her sister had told her, before she could even start to extract further shreds of truth from out of her sibling's failing body, before she could fully make sense of anything, there were frenzied shouts and screeches from servants. It was now certain they had not fled the *palazzo*. But what was this? Zeta had fallen? But worse, a daughter of the house too! Mafalda was experiencing the first agonizing symptoms of the Black Death? Both of them mothers to the child, Lagia and Mirella turned into each other's eyes afeard and searching for hope. But as for hope, neither had any.

Tonia

How a handful of poisonous fungi had made its way into the weekly delivery of mushrooms for the house was a mystery. Certainly, it had been an accident. A picker on *terra firma* making a mistake about what was edible, and what was not. Perhaps the few that had made it into the basket delivered to Orso's house were not the only poisoned mushrooms to be delivered around the city; other Venetians might have also eaten them and become sick. Or perhaps Paola and Tonia had been the only ones.

The cook had minced a good bunch of mushrooms together. With onion and garlic, herbs and chopped pine nuts, hand pies with such an aromatic filling were baked. It was just as they had cooled that Paola had returned with Tonia from the market, both refreshed by the chilly sea air and sun. They both entered the kitchen together and were met with the delicious smell of garlicky mushrooms. Alas, the cook forbade Tonia to eat a pie. They were strictly for the family. Paola took one, but after placing down a basket of fruit for the cook, did leave the kitchen so as not to eat before Tonia. To tease her would be unkind.

That night, she'd had fitful nightmares and had

dampened her bed with sweat. The next day she felt clammy and had a slight headache, and so did not eat much. But on the following day, she craved another helping of mushroom pie. Was there any left? Why yes, left in a cool place in the larder, the pies had yet gone untouched apart from the one she'd had before. And so Paola ate another, and suffered more for some days, and was lucky when she didn't die. Though it eventually had become obvious that she had been poisoned, no one ever guessed rightly where the toxin had come from.

Even as the girl recovered, Tonia discovered what was left of the pies, preserved quite nicely in a cool dark place. Usually any pie, whether made of vegetables or meat, fruit or fish, did not last but a day or two in such a busy house. But these had. What luck for Tonia! One after the other, Tonia finished the hand pies while she worked in the kitchen, and died that very evening. Not only had she been a thief of pies, but also of small treasures. Didn't she deserve small comforts as much as any noble girl, for she worked hard, and was mostly good. But it was embarrassing that those candies from Paola's room should have been found in her hand at her death, proof of her filching ways.

She could never have guessed what was coming. Her stomach had hurt some, and she'd felt a bit too warm and had wanted to lie down. But there was still work yet to be done. A few lemon confections would help her through! Yet before one had even made it into her mouth, terrible pains struck her and a fit so terrible, that she was brought to her knees. No one could know how long she'd suffered there on that stone floor. It might have been an hour, two even, before Paola found her.

In her last moments, though they were terrible, Paola had uttered prayers straight to God's ear. In life, she'd been a servant. But as darkness fell over her sight, and she took her last breath, she was granted passage into a bright place without burden.

Mirella

As she bowed her head, knees perched upon a soft cushioned stool, her elbows resting easily atop her bed in prayer, Mirella felt overwhelmed by pain and guilt. To learn that her daughters had been her sister's children had been so incomprehensible, as to be barely believed. All along, Mirella had assumed that Orso had grown bored of fidelity. That he'd had other women amidst his travels, yielding children that she was expected to care for. That he'd felt disdain that she could not offer him a child. But rather, each time a babe had been delivered into her arms, it had been both Orso's way of helping her poor sister while giving a precious gift to his wife. Orso had wanted Mirella to be happy. He'd never even told a soul that the children had not been hers. Had done everything in his power so that the world would believe that they were. Tried to take away the pressures she must have been feeling among the women. Had even taken her away for extended trips to be given her children, so that no one would question it.

Mirella knew now that Orso had been a faithful man to her all along. He'd been a saint even! He'd tried to make past wrongs right, had loved his wife, and had taken in children not of his own blood to raise them as his own. Oh, what had she done? She'd chosen Thorello, one of Orso's men to do it. She had bribed him with a great sum. Thorello had traveled with the other men on that last expedition, all of whom had claimed surprise when Orso did not make it back to Venice before they had. None of them knew that Thorello *had* encountered their master.

He'd planned it well. As the party took their ease at an inn on a daylong break in their journey, Thorello asserted that he had business in a small village further along. He would meet up with them the following day as they rode onward. Thorello had not had business however, but rather a grim commission. He knew that Orso was not far ahead of the pack, and galloped out to catch up with him on the road. Later, he nodded to Mirella that it had been done. It had been easier too, than he'd expected. He hadn't even needed to draw his sword. As he rode up behind him just aside a crumbling stone bridge along the path, Thorello caught Orso unawares. With a mighty push he'd knocked him from off his mount, and Mirella's stout husband fell over the edge, crashing upon rocks below. There was no way that he could have survived the fall. And anyone to come upon his body would suspect that the noble had *fallen* from his horse while riding past the bridge. It was unlikely that the noble's identity would even be discovered, for Thorello had dispatched of the man's saddlebag, and had startled Orso's horse more than it already was to set it running.

But just now as she murmured with eyes drawn tightly closed, she remembered how Thorello had carried Paola to her room when the girl had fallen ill. How gently he'd carried her, and how gingerly he'd placed her into bed. Had it been pity for a now fatherless girl, and he the murderer? Or had he a secret? Perhaps he'd met Orso on the road, but only to warn the man of his wife's plot against him. Mirella now believed that this might very well be possible. Those poisoned lemon candies amongst her last chest of gifts, perhaps even forwarded to her on the very day Thorello warned her husband, had marked her as a target of his fury. Was Orso still alive and in hiding? Would he eventually seek her out when the plague subsided, and find a way to murder her for her sins against him? All in due time. Mirella gasped at a sudden noise and glanced suspiciously around her room. Thorello may not even be alive anymore, with what had befallen the city. But even if she had the opportunity to question him in secret, there would be no way of knowing the real truth. Only Orso and Thorello really knew what had transpired on the road. All Mirella could do was wait. But whether he'd died, or whether he returned, she'd already damned herself. How black her future, how full of despair! Oh, Orso!

Lagia. Her sister was now gone. After their spell before the fire, Mirella saturating every word she spoke, they'd heard the commotion outside of the chamber. All of those servants, who had before seemed so hidden, had scurried out into the halls with a hurry. Lagia had remained unmoving where she sat, and did not dart out into the hall with her. Zeta was dying on Mafalda's floor, and her daughter had just collapsed near the kitchen. Both girls were certain to have the plague. The night had been long, and it broke her to witness Mafalda's terrible pain and delirium. With all of the recent revelations, Mirella's grief was even more amplified to see her child suffering so. How she wished that she could turn back time and show each of her girls the boundless love that is a parent's. But as the dawn came, it was certain that she had lost one of them forever. A bell was soon rung in the *calle* for a *beccamorto*. Zeta's body was removed first, and then Mafalda's.

As Mirella, stunned and exhausted, finally

reentered her room those long hours later, she found Lagia still sitting in the same place. She hadn't even been moved to come out and catch a glimpse of one of her children? Had she fallen asleep? Puzzled, Mirella soon saw that the woman was deathly still as she walked near. Lagia had passed away in the night. In as many years as her sister had fought her disease, the time had finally come and her body could not fight it any more. Mirella called for a servant to catch the *beccamorto*. There was yet another body to take. Who would be next?

In that moment, she'd suddenly felt the urge to go to Orso's meeting chamber. She was in search of something, though she didn't know if she would find it. She was looking for his orders, his manifests for the *palazzo*. In these last months, how many vendors with orders for Orso had arrived! But why? Why had her husband asked for these things?

She hurried out of her room toward his, anguished and near collapse. After sifting, and scanning, she eventually found what she was looking for, written in his hand. A list. *Gifts for my wife...to be presented on the anniversary of our 25th nuptial day*. Why hadn't she suspected before? The gondola, the jewelry, the fabrics, and the many other fine goods that she'd sent back, the orders she'd canceled. As she read through each item on the list, every new present was a dagger stab to her heart. And there, where she'd found the list, another similar paper, one with instructions. Orso had been planning to host a feast in honor of their many years together. And all the while, she'd been planning his exit from the world.

What should she do now? How could she live another day after learning all? After she had committed such sins against her own family? There was only one way to work toward some kind of redemption. As soon as it could be permitted, she would voluntarily submit herself into a nunnery. If she did not die of this plague, she would live out her days in solitude and prayer, albeit a life even better than she deserved.

The Garden II.

On a warm morning in late spring, the ladies lounged upon a rooftop terrace. It was no dream, but in the flesh. Only this garden towered at the top of a new home, over their city just finally clear of the plague. Aurelia had died in the terrible siege, but had had the saintly kindness to think of her friend at her very end. She'd hastily scratched out a sentence with a shaking quill, dripping ink in every place. Her signature was the last word she ever wrote. It was because of this loving gesture that Fina had inherited Aurelia's *palazzo* and all that it had contained, ensuring that she would forever have a home. Fina thought of her and smiled each and every day while traveling its halls. How much she missed her bold and beautiful friend.

There had been another inheritance as well, far greater and more unexpected. Just as the plague began to sputter out, Mirella quickly began selling a great many fine possessions, and then their house. Soon after, she had entered a nunnery. All of the money she'd reaped was immediately bequeathed to her four daughters. Now wealthy and independent, they were choosing to live as they would, without intervention. For each, it was a new chance at happiness.

Mafalda had remained with Fina during her long recovery, and then never left after Aurelia bestowed Fina her dwelling. It was there that they'd received the blessed news of Noemi's whereabouts and safety, and of her quiet wedding to Ilario, a maker of gondolas that their father had once hired. They'd but bowed their heads before a priest, alone amidst the echoes and shadows inside one of Venice's ancient churches. Noemi's older sisters could not have been more comforted and elated to learn of it.

Today, on this beautiful sunny day, Mafalda stood and bounced a precious young girl in her arms, who she had named Pearl. Soon sitting down with the tired nestling, she softly sang...

Gone and lost my precious pearl?
Hast thou passed out through my door?
I shall not live if you're not with me.
Boatman, boatman, swiftly.
Bring her back, and quickly.
Bring her back...
My breaking heart to speed thyne oar...

The melody was soothing and the words were sweet, even if they were sad. She could remember now the minstrel from whose lips she'd heard it first, though he had been no court musician at all.

Baldovino had warbled it from a gondola one night out below on the canal. Mafalda had watched him from her window, a pearl dangling over the edge and glinting in the light of the moon. He'd given her the prettiest of pearls, but also, the far more beloved one that now rocked in her arms.

Fina lounged close-by in a wooden chair, her long hair growing out, returning to its darker hue. She smiled as she took in the sun and the blue sky above. A verbal cat swirled around her feet. She'd taken in a few cats, two parrots, and a tiny skittish dog. It had brought life to the *palazzo*, but the animals had also been homeless on account of so many losses during the plague. More and more, Aurelia's fine house was becoming one of the most cheerful and comfortable homes in *Venezia*, while outside, the city was finally starting to heal.

And there, stood Noemi, visiting for the morning. She'd brought them all fresh strawberries from the market. She was gazing out over Venice from their great height. Clinging vines thickly dangled from a trellis above her head. She looked like a Greek goddess as the greenery blew around her flashing curls, while dressed in a long plain gown and lovingly rubbing her growing belly.

And though Paola was not with them, they discussed her letters and marveled at her adventures. Their youngest sister's many stories seemed nearly unbelievable, but were certainly true. After jumping from a high window, not greatly injured, she'd hobbled through the maze of *calli* back to the House of Orso, fearless of anyone she might encounter while treading all alone on the streets. She was determined to confront her mother, and was shocked by the way she was so emotionally embraced when she did. Mirella vowed that she had never lifted a hand to hurt her. She'd never fed her poison. When seeing the sincerity in her mother's eyes, Paola had believed her. And yet, though she tried withal, leaving the mystery behind her would ever prove difficult.

Thankfully, no one else in that great house had taken ill, nor would again while the pestilence continued. Paola had remained by Mirella's side as their mother eventually sold a great many goods and emptied the house. She had respected their mother's desire to enter a nunnery without question, never knowing what her full reasons might be. The loss of Orso, and all that had transpired in *Venezia*, seemed to have altered her. As if overnight, she had grown patient, kind and devout. One day, Mirella asked for

Paola's forgiveness, and in turn, the forgiveness of each of her children. Such conversations were brief and vague, as Mirella uttered apologies for lost time, and for the painful way they'd all parted. But it was something. She even began to quietly encourage her youngest to travel away from Venice, as the child had always so desired. However, with such backing, she did make Paola promise to return after she'd seen all that she needed to see. Paola should come home, to her sisters and to her city, for she was a beloved child of Venice. Giving her gold enough to last her on her journey, they eventually parted ways with ample tears.

With a razed head and clothed in leathers, a cloak and a sword, the fearless young woman had left home by posing as a man. After making her way to land, she traveled on by horseback, riding for long stretches each day. At night, she slept in any village, farm or field. Wherever she deemed safe. Paola was now a woman wayfarer, gone to see the world. What an odyssey she would return to tell. Even now, she had just passed out of Hungary into Wallachia; it could hardly be imagined. Though awed by her strength and courage, the youth's mother and sisters continually prayed for her safety. Such a journey by a woman was as perilous as it was unprecedented.

And though their mother did not join them that day upon the rooftop garden, to laugh and smile and love her children and grandchildren, born and unborn, she was praying and loving them from her place, stitching beautiful things for them, and singing hymns of deliverance, thankfulness and humility. Each in turn, her daughters forgave her their hurts, and never forsook her. Of course, they had no knowledge of her greatest crime. Of that, Mirella only ever spoke to God.

All together, they often went to visit her before the grates of the convent foyer, on all feast days and each Sunday. They brought her books and rich things to eat, and held hands with her through the bars. Not a visit passed that Mirella didn't shed tears, thankful that her past bitterness and inattention hadn't taken root in the hearts of her children. Her misdeeds had not ruined their chances for free and fruitful futures. Just as the city of Venice had irrevocably changed, so too had the House of Orso.